TO SNARE A SPY

Jon Stock read English at Cambridge University and worked for many years at *The Daily Telegraph*, as a foreign correspondent in New Delhi and as editor of the Saturday Weekend section. He is the author of five spy thrillers, including *Dead Spy Running*, which was optioned by Warner Bros.

Writing as J.S. Monroe, Jon is also the author of *Find Me*, a psychological thriller published in the UK and America. Translation rights have been sold to more than ten countries.

Jon lives in Wiltshire with his wife Hilary, a fine art photographer who exhibits at the Harbour Gallery in Portscatho, and their three children, all of whom are regular visitors to Cornwall.

Follow Jon Stock @JSThrillers

By the same author

The Riot Act
The Cardamom Club
Dead Spy Running
Games Traitors Play
Dirty Little Secret

Writing as J.S. Monroe

Find Me

TO SNARE A SPY

A SHORT THRILLER SET ON THE
SOUTH COAST OF CORNWALL

Jon Stock

Published by The Nare Hotel Co. Ltd 2017

This novel is a work of fiction and the product of the author's imagination. Many readers will, however, recognise a number of authentic Cornish settings and places. Real people and businesses also feature, but the roles they all play in this story are entirely fictitious.

9 7 5 3 1 2 4 6 8

First published in the UK in 2017 by
The Nare Hotel Co. Ltd
Carne Beach
Veryan-in-Roseland
Cornwall TR2 5PF
www.narehotel.co.uk
www.tosnareaspy.com
01872 501111

The Nare Hotel Company Ltd. Reg. No. 02323722

ISBN (HB): 978 0 9561108 1 7
ISBN (PB): 978 0 9561108 2 4
ISBN (E): 978 0 9561108 3 1

Typeset by Averill Buchanan
in 11pt on 14.5pt Minion

Produced in Great Britain by
TJ INK, www.tjink.co.uk,
part of TJ International - Quality Book Manufacturers,
Padstow, Cornwall.

For all the staff at The Nare

Publisher's Preface

WHENEVER JON STOCK visits us in Cornwall I always have to allow my imagination to change into the fifth gear of espionage. I believe the first occasion I met Jon, Hilary and their fun-loving family was when helping to research some detail for Jon's 2011 spy thriller *Games Traitors Play*. It was prior to his appointment at the *Telegraph* as Executive Head of Life and Weekend – the coolest business card in town – and I was clearly briefed by our PR team at Wild West to host this important journalist/writer and provide the background scenario for the opening scene of his new book. The challenge, to land – realistically and without suspicion – a spy off a Russian tanker anchored in Falmouth Bay onto the rocks under St Anthony Head, was well within the remit of an ex-naval officer turned independent hotelier. We used the hotel's Cornish Crabber to get in close underneath the cliffs, where we contrived a storyline that would allow for a Search and Rescue helicopter from RNAS Culdrose to be hijacked.

A couple of bottles of Taittinger in The Goring cocktail bar and a few years later, the pace had quickened. The hotel's recently acquired classic motor launch was pushing twenty knots as she narrowly missed Black Rock at the entrance to Carrick Roads under the cover of darkness. The Ashworth and Stock families were returning from the Helford River where conversation had turned to grandfather's wartime stories of a suspicious-looking SOE maritime operations vessel, masquerading as a Breton fishing trawler, that had been seen heading off around The Manacles... The ingredients of another short thriller were emerging.

'There's never a dull moment running an hotel' is a favourite family saying of ours and one that is reasonably well justified, given the hundred-odd years that the family has been running hotels in Cornwall. As you can imagine, there are many stories to be told. Hotels are fascinating places where different characters, guests and staff come together in an intoxicating social mix that reveals extraordinary backgrounds and contacts. The serenity and comfort of the front of house counterpoints beautifully with the behind-the-scenes passion and determination to ensure that all is provided for guests. It is this fine balance that makes running hotels such a buzz – and why they make the perfect backdrop for spy thrillers.

Thus I am sure that John le Carré, when writing *The Night Manager*, and Jon Stock, the author of this book, found that hotels have real people who work in them, each with their own riveting back story –or should that be cover story? Hidden and surprising talents found amongst staff in any hotel should not be overlooked, particularly by an author in search of a good tale. While researching this book, our own writer-in-residence discovered that we have, in our midst, staff who have experience in forensic science, MI5, naval intelligence, airline security, international shipping and piracy. Add an injection of Russian-Latvian political experience and the plot starts to thicken.

This book unashamedly celebrates these people. Please be aware, however, that there are other characters whose names and stories we should not wholly believe. After all, when operating in the shadowy world of espionage, one can never really tell who is on which side. So it is probably just best to sit back and enjoy the story. And if you like it, our well-stocked library has all of Jon's other spy novels.

Another essential and very real ingredient of this book is the stunning local coastal scenery. There are beautiful old churches, areas and waterways of outstanding natural beauty which are found on and around the Roseland Peninsula and the Fal and Helford rivers. They have borne witness to significant historical wartime events, including recently uncovered feats of espionage, and create an inspirational and natural environment in which to stage a spy thriller.

One final point. It has come to light that Noah and Clemmie, the hero and heroine of this book, did not in fact accomplish all that they set out to find. They have left unfinished business, as well as evidence of their first mission (including a letter hidden in the hotel). *To Snare a Spy* should therefore be seen as background briefing for future SOE insertions and spy operations that will require further agents to follow in their footsteps. In short, there will be opportunities aplenty in the future for aspiring spooks staying at The Nare to be recruited and go undercover as agents, completing Noah and Clemmie's original mission.

Every business should have a 'fund for fun' and this book certainly dips into that fund at The Nare. However, it should be seen not just as a piece of novel marketing but also as well-deserved recognition and heartfelt thanks for all the hard work that our staff put towards making every guest staying at The Nare feel comfortable.

Spy master contact for agents: telephone 01872 500007, or visit www.tosnareaspy.com/spooks

Toby Ashworth
Proprietor, The Nare
Cornwall
Spring 2017

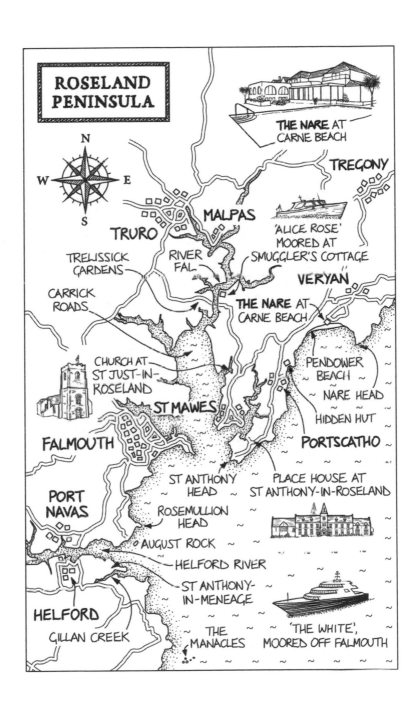

1

NOAH LOOKED UP and down the empty hotel corridor and knew at once that something was wrong. Leaning in towards the crack of the door, he searched for a single strand of his own dark hair that he had left there an hour earlier. It was an old tradecraft trick but still effective.

Where was it? He had trapped the hair between the door and its frame before going downstairs to join his parents for dinner on the Quarterdeck. *Breathe.* Someone had tried to enter the room in his absence and dislodged the hair. Was someone following him?

He checked the number: 15. It was the right room.

He pushed open the door, pulse quickening. Someone *had* been here. He walked over to the small, single-bed cabin off his parents' room where he had slept every summer holiday since he could remember. His bedspread was turned back, pyjamas folded neatly for the first time since last summer. Housekeeping.

Noah sank down on the bed, running his hands through his hair as he contemplated what lay ahead of him in the next few days. If he was going to succeed, he needed to be calmer and avoid 'catastrophising', as his housemaster called it. He walked back into his parents' room, sat down on a sofa and stared out to sea. *Relax.* Tomorrow he would hang out around the hotel while his parents went out: go down to Carne Beach, read, swim in the pool, maybe play some tennis.

It was no good. He leant forward and flicked through some copies of *Cornwall Today*, *Tatler* and *Country Living*, fanned out like a deck of large cards on the glass table. It should be feeling like the holidays, but it didn't. Not this time. Standing up, he slid back the glass door and stepped out onto the balcony. A warm wind ruffled the leaves of two palm trees below him.

A couple of days ago he'd been packing his school bags for the summer break, the first two weeks of which were always spent down here in Cornwall. It was as he was struggling to zip up his bulging suitcase that Alexei, his Russian roommate, had cleared his throat and said something so strange, so beyond the bounds of their everyday banter, that he had sensed his life might never be the same again.

'Are you a patriot, Noah?'

'How do you mean?' Noah had carried on tussling with the zip, trying to ignore the question. 'Give me a hand, will you?'

Alexei came over to sit on the suitcase like a victorious wrestler. 'Do you love your country?' he asked.

Noah paused for a moment, unclear where the conversation was going. It was not uncommon for Alexei to wax lyrical about his motherland – his father was a senior member of the Russian government – but his tone was usually light, his chatter full of funny asides. Only the day before he had spoken about going hunting with his dad for capercaillie near the White Sea, on the southern edge of the Arctic Circle. 'He wouldn't accept that I was a man until I'd shot one,' Alexei had joked. Today, though, his manner was different, full of foreboding.

'I don't like the British weather much,' Noah said, still in denial. 'I think this zip's knackered.'

'I'm not joking.'

Noah looked up at Alexei, who slid off the suitcase and walked over to the window, his hands thrust deep into the pockets of his

Savile Row suit. He was tall, one of the tallest in the house, and always seemed to dress older than his years, perhaps in an attempt to compensate for his baby-faced good looks.

Noah turned back to his suitcase again, worried by the seriousness that now filled their small room like a dense fog.

'I like Cornwall—'

'I love my country very much, Noah,' Alexei interrupted, pacing around the room, clearly irritated by his friend's insouciance.

'I know you do.' Noah paused. '"The motherland."'

'But it's gone to the dogs.'

'I'm sure your father's doing all he can to—'

'He's trying, but it's difficult. Very dangerous. He plays the game, of course, the double life. In public, he's loyal, but secretly he despises Putin. Many of his government colleagues think the same, but what can they do? Putin is a powerful man.' Alexei's voice faltered. 'I love my father. He needs help, Noah. From someone like you.'

'Me?' Noah couldn't disguise his surprise.

'Why not?' Alexei paused. 'Do you know what it's like to have a famous father?'

Noah didn't. His dad was a faceless civil servant – a number-cruncher at the Office for National Statistics in London. Noah loved him, but they weren't close. A combination of his dad's long working hours and Noah having been sent away to a Scottish boarding school had left their relationship more distant than Noah would have liked. He sensed his dad felt the same too.

'When your father is someone important, you have no idea who your real friends are, why people are being so nice to you,' Alexei continued. 'But you were a friend to me from our first day here together, before you knew who my father was. You told me to never let a rugby ball bounce. You explained how to bypass the school internet filters with web proxies. And how to talk to English girls. I will never forget that.'

3

'No problem.' Noah smiled at the memory of Alexei catching the rugby ball after kick-off and running away from the opposition as they charged towards him. 'Wrong way!' his teammates had all shouted. 'Are you joking?' Alexei had said as he sped towards his own touchline.

'And I trust you,' Alexei continued.

Noah had grown fond of Alexei over the past year, but there was something about his adult tone of voice that was beginning to scare him. For a moment, they just stood there, in silence, looking at each other.

'President Putin has an ally in your country's government,' Alexei announced.

'An ally?'

'A "mole", I think you say. Someone who is betraying Britain and working for Putin. A traitor. *Izmennik*. Someone very senior in the British establishment.'

'You've finally been reading Le Carré then,' Noah said, glancing at his bookshelves. It was John le Carré, after all, who had coined the term 'mole', which was later adopted by the real-life intelligence services. Noah's tone was throwaway, but Alexei had got his attention. First a renegade politician in Moscow, now a Russian mole in London. He'd only ever read about these things.

Noah was obsessed with spy fiction, had been from an unnaturally early age. His favourite book was *The Spy Who Came in from the Cold*. 'Plot like a Swiss watch,' he had told Alexei on their first day, trying to persuade him to read it.

He loved spy films too, particularly James Bond (although he identified more with Q than 007), and he even ran his own espionage website. Forget Hamleys. Mayfair's spy shops were more his bag.

'I wish it was fiction, but it's not,' Alexei said. 'This mole could make life very difficult for my father. There are many in Moscow who would like to reach out to Britain for help – my father and

4

his friends cannot remove Putin on their own. But this mole? He would get to hear of any talk of regime change.'

'Which is why Putin put him there.'

'He's clever. How else do you think he has survived as president for so long? You're going to Cornwall soon, no? To that smart hotel you're always telling me about? Where they set fire to their puddings?'

Noah nodded.

'Then you can help, my friend – your country and mine. I'll be in touch very soon.'

And that's how Alexei had left it. A real-life spy story lobbed into the calm waters of his fantasy world of espionage.

It wasn't until Noah had unpacked his suitcase in his hotel room before dinner that he'd found the letter from Alexei. His friend must have slipped it into his luggage when he was helping him zip it up.

Noah turned to his bedside table and retrieved the letter. It was handwritten, describing a rare recent visit to his home, a grand tsarist-era dacha in a pine forest outside Moscow (Alexei was always showing Noah photos on his phone). And it outlined in measured detail what Noah needed to do if he wished to 'help' Britain – and help the real motherland of Russia.

My dear crazy British friend Noah,

By the time you read this, I hope you are already in Cornwall with your family. I wish I was in Moscow now with mine, but sadly it cannot be because of visa complications.

The day after you arrive in Cornwall, a Russian oligarch, former KGB, will visit Falmouth on his yacht. His name is Oleg Borisovich Kreshensky and the yacht is called The White. *You cannot miss it: it's ninety metres long and five storeys high. Kreshensky is close to Putin – why else do you think he is allowed to keep his Western luxuries? – and likes to refer to himself as 'The Admiral'. He surrounds himself with friends and cronies, all of them Putin poodles, but he is the only one the President trusts to run the mole. He is his 'handler'.*

On my last trip home to Moscow (when I told you I was visiting my guardian in Manchester – apologies for lying), my father held a dinner party for some government colleagues who share his views about Putin. I joined them for a while – my father likes to show me off to his friends, now that I have shot my first capercaillie – before I was told to make myself scarce, which means playing Call of Duty *in my bedroom. The wives were sent out too. (Before you say anything, this is Russia and we still do things differently here, OK?!)*

I have spent a lot of my childhood sitting at the top of the stairs, listening to my parents' dinner parties, and that night was no exception. I crept out of my room and could only catch bits of their conversation above the music (Tchaikovsky, of course – my father's favourite), but what I heard sounded very important.

There appears to be an issue with a member of Kreshensky's staff. His butler has been working for him for many years, but he is disillusioned and has started to behave erratically. The man has a Latvian girlfriend working in England and is upset that he has not been allowed to see her for a long time – Kreshensky won't let him leave the boat when they are in the UK. This is where you, my friend, can help. The girlfriend works as a waitress at a country-house hotel by the sea in Cornwall – I believe it is the same one where you always stay and are now, I hope, reading this letter.

This unhappy butler is your key to identifying the mole, who is due to meet up with Kreshensky in secret when he visits Cornwall. I have not told my father any of this and I risk my life by telling you, but I want to help him. You will risk your life if you tell others what you are doing. Do not go public on your spy website until you are certain of the mole's identity. And be careful: intelligence services are very protective – they prefer their moles to stay underground, away from daylight. I have no doubt our own SVR will be watching, listening.

> *My mad British roommate, I know this all sounds*
> *like one of your spy books, but it's true and you must be*
> *brave – be a man. This is your capercaillie moment! Act*
> *now if you love your country and mine and, please, no*
> *joke, destroy this letter after you have read it.*

Noah put down the sheet of paper, stood up and walked around the hotel room. He didn't feel very brave right now. And he had no intention of destroying the letter. Not yet. He also knew that Alexei wasn't bluffing. The SVR, Russia's external intelligence agency (successors to the KGB's First Chief Directorate), kept a close eye on Alexei at their school in Scotland.

During his first term, Alexei had joined the Combined Cadet Force, wearing army uniform and practising drills on a Monday afternoon. The SVR, who must have been watching from beyond the school gates, contacted his father in Moscow, asking him if he was aware that his son had just signed up to the Royal Regiment of Scotland, a core component of the British Army. His father went ballistic (worried, no doubt, what Putin would think) and rang Alexei, who had to resign from the CCF and take up voluntary work on Mondays instead, visiting local residential homes.

Noah continued pacing around the room. Would his parents notice if he had a slug of sherry from the decanter next to the TV? Probably. His dad had a sixth sense about such things.

He looked out of the hotel window. To the west, Portscatho, to the east, Nare Head. Before he'd gone downstairs for dinner, he'd downloaded *Marine Traffic*, an app that used the automatic identification system (AIS) to track the position, speed and destination of ships. He'd been following the Russian yacht ever since. *The White* was due to arrive in Falmouth tonight, having spent several days moored alongside HMS *Belfast* in London before making its way down the Channel.

According to Google, Kreshensky lived in Moscow and had financial interests in a number of UK businesses, including a

Midlands football club. He brought his yacht over to the UK once a year, for a month of cruising along the coastline.

Noah thought about the challenge that lay ahead of him, the opportunity to put all that he'd read about espionage into practice. He was no fan of Putin and admired Alexei's dad for standing up to him, however secretly. His first task was to get himself on board and talk to the butler, find out if Kreshensky had any plans to come ashore. It was a long shot, but Alexei had stressed that the butler was his key to identifying the mole. The hotel employed a number of Eastern European staff, from Latvia, Romania and Slovakia. He just needed to establish which one had a Russian boyfriend working on a Russian oligarch's superyacht.

He picked up his night-vision binoculars, a birthday present from his grandpa, and scanned the horizon. A couple of container ships were anchored off Falmouth, waiting for their turn to dock. Beyond them loomed an oil tanker, also at anchor. 'Third-largest natural deep-water harbour in the world,' as his grandpa was always telling him. And then he saw it: the sleek white profile of a ninety-metre superyacht, sliding across the horizon on its way towards Falmouth. He tried to bring it into focus, but his hands were shaking too much.

2

NOT FOR THE first time in his life, Noah woke too late to join his parents for breakfast. It wasn't that he was lazy – he sometimes felt he had too much energy. The clock in his head was calibrated differently, that was all. He liked to rise late and go to bed late. 'BTT – British teenage time,' his mum joked. She had slipped a note under his cabin door, explaining that they had driven over to the Lost Gardens of Heligan with his grandpa for the morning and would be back for a late lunch.

He hoped they were having a good time, although he was surprised his dad had gone too – he'd never shown much interest in gardening as far as Noah was aware. It would be a bonus if this holiday brought his dad out of his shell a bit, he thought. He was always tired and seemed worn down by his job, the world. Sometimes Noah wondered if he was ashamed of his career, given how little he spoke about it. They could only afford to stay at this hotel each summer because his grandpa came with them and picked up the bill. His grandpa – 'ninety-four-years young', as he liked to tell all the waitresses – paid for Noah's private school in Scotland too, the school to which his dad had won a full scholarship in the sixth form.

Noah showered, dressed and went downstairs, where he had some coffee and a croissant on the Quarterdeck. Thank God for the late risers' continental breakfast, he thought. There was no one else in the dining room, but he could hear a lot of activity up by the reception desk.

'What's that all about?' Noah asked the young waitress who refilled his coffee cup.

'A VIP's arriving today,' she said. Noah noted a faint Cornish accent.

'Jay Z?' he asked, grinning.

'Not quite. Jack MacKenzie, the new Home Secretary.'

Noah almost choked on his coffee. He put his cup down on the saucer. 'Is he coming with his family?' he asked, mopping up the spill with his linen napkin.

'Just his daughter. He lost his wife a couple of years ago.'

I know, Noah thought.

'They come every year, apparently,' the waitress continued. 'I've only just started here. First time he's been back as Home Secretary, though. His security people are checking out his rooms right now. The Pendower Suite, of course.'

Noah sat in silence, stunned by the news. *Just his daughter*. Just Clemmie. Clementine bloody MacKenzie. The most beautiful girl in his school. The love of his life. He wished.

Clemmie was in the year above, and most of the boys, and quite a few girls, were in love with her. In addition to her classic good looks – bleached blonde hair, full lips, freckles, cupric green eyes – she had just played a stunning Sandy in the school production of *Grease*. She captained the girls' football team (and was probably good enough to captain the boys' team too) and was expected to get eleven A*s in her GCSEs, even though she had seemingly not done a stroke of work.

She was also permanently in trouble for wearing too short a skirt and being caught drinking on school nights, but she had never been suspended or expelled. Maybe it was because she'd lost her mother. Or because her father was tipped for the very highest of government jobs. Either way, she was a living example of how to be a bit bad and very good at the same time. And she was single. No one had ever said as much, but Noah assumed that her legion of admirers had concluded, like him, that they would fall too far short of her high standards to make it even worth trying.

'Are you OK?' the waitress asked, concerned.

'Fine,' Noah said. The waitress smiled at him as she cleared his side plate. He was desperate to text Clemmie but didn't wish to appear rude. The hotel discouraged the use of mobiles in public places, much to the delight of his parents, who were always telling him to get off his phone.

'Holiday job?' he asked.

'Yeah. I'm at uni. My three brothers worked here before me. Parents live up the road at Tregony.'

'Where are you studying?'

'Bournemouth.'

'Doing what? Hospitality?'

'Forensic science.'

'No way. That's cool.' Noah didn't quite know what to say, where to go with this surprising information, as he folded and unfolded his napkin. 'DNA testing, that sort of thing?'

'Blood groups at crime scenes, human or animal, cause of death.'

Noah looked at the waitress again, impressed. Never be deceived by an innocent face, he told himself.

'I'm specialising in blood spatter,' she added.

'Now you're ripping me,' Noah said, but he had a feeling she wasn't.

Before he had reached his room, Noah was messaging Clemmie on Snapchat.

'You said you weren't coming to Cornwall this year...?' he wrote. She was meant to be in Ibiza by now, with the rest of her year, celebrating the end of GCSEs.

She messaged back straight away.

'Yeah, change of plan… Can't tell anyone what we're doing these days aha ;) Dad's orders.'

'Oh aha… so mysterious ;) When are you arriving?'

'Here already. Dad coming down tonight. Do you want to meet?'

Did he want to meet? He knew he should play hard to get, say that he was busy, but there was nothing he would rather do in the world right then than meet up with Clemmie MacKenzie. Away from school, she seemed more attainable somehow. He was aware that he was punching way above his weight, but that mattered less down here in Cornwall, far from the classroom cliques and peer pressure.

At least, it hadn't mattered last year, when they'd kissed in the hotel hot tub, late one night, beside the outdoor swimming pool, looking out at a low full moon that had lit up the sea like a searchlight.

'Sure,' he typed.

It had just been a kiss, never acknowledged since, let alone repeated, but she had smiled afterwards and he could still taste her lips twelve months later.

3

'SO, MR SPY MAN,' Clemmie said in her soft Edinburgh burr, 'I could get you a job with MI5 now that my dad's Home Secretary.'

'GCHQ's more my thing,' Noah said. 'Better gadgets. Thanks all the same, though.'

They were walking west towards Portscatho along a grassy coastpath that had been grazed as short as a golf green by five Dartmoor ponies who wandered freely during the summer months. One of them was up ahead, eyeing them nonchalantly. Not a bad life, Noah thought. Beneath them a wind was whipping up the sea, white waves flashing in the bright summer sunshine. A kite-surfer carved a solitary path across the bay; two women rode horses on the sand. The tide was out and the beach was a playground, full of families and dogs on leads, but they had both wanted to go for a walk.

'How long are you here for?' Noah asked, keen to calculate the number of days he had to win her over.

Clemmie said nothing as she negotiated a stile in her tight denim shorts and walked on ahead.

'Oh, come on,' Noah said. 'Who am I going to tell?'

'No idea. That's the problem with you,' she said, now beside the Dartmoor pony and stroking it. Noah remembered that she

13

was good with horses, a keen rider. The one time he'd tried to commune with a pony it had bolted. 'My dad wasn't too pleased when I told him I might be seeing Noah Standing down here.'

'You're kidding me?' Noah didn't know whether to laugh or cry. He thought he'd got on well with her father on the only occasion they'd met, at the hotel this time last year. Admittedly, the Home Secretary was from Edinburgh, whereas his dad was from Glasgow, but no one was perfect.

'The powers that be weren't too impressed with all that publicity you gave Edward Snowden,' she continued.

'Publicity? My website gets a thousand page-views a month, if I'm lucky. Not exactly BuzzFeed.'

He felt simultaneously flattered and scared that his nascent site had already caught the attention of the 'powers that be', whoever they were. GCHQ, he hoped. He dreamt of working at 'the Doughnut', their circular steel offices in the suburbs of Cheltenham. He'd recently bought a book of GCHQ puzzles and had cracked almost all of them.

First, though, he needed to persuade his dad to let him apply for a place at the National College of Cyber Security, a brand-new boarding school for gifted coders. Appropriately enough, it was to be located at Block G in Bletchley Park, the famous Second World War Enigma code-breaking centre near Milton Keynes. The first intake was slated for 2018: he would make a point of talking to his dad about it over the next couple of weeks.

'Anyway, I didn't take sides on Snowden,' Noah added, thinking back to his posts about the American's controversial mass-data-gathering revelations. 'Just reported the facts, said what he'd done, posed the big question: freedom fighter or enemy of the state?'

'He betrayed the West,' Clemmie said. 'That's what he did. According to Dad, anyway. Made life more difficult for our spies.'

'Did I say he didn't?'

'Hero or villain, then?'

'Good and bad. Just like all of us.' Noah smiled at Clemmie, who returned the compliment and took his hand.

'I like you,' she said, swinging his arm theatrically as if to defuse the sudden intimacy between them. 'I like the way you didn't give a damn what people thought of you when you arrived at school.'

Noah had joined in the fourth form, ten months earlier. It hadn't been a smooth entry. There were already too many tightly knit friendship groups, not to mention a well-established social hierarchy based on sport and a macho lads' culture. The strangest bit had been the way girls and boys seemed not to interact. His previous school was a mixed state academy in London, where the sexes mingled freely and he had been very happy. After a year of parental pressure, however, he had agreed to move. His dad had wanted Noah to have the advantages that he'd enjoyed, though his mum had been less keen.

At his new private school in Scotland, which followed the English system, it wasn't the boarding that bothered him, more the dining hall. Boys sat on one side, girls on the other. There was no rule; that's just how it was – until he walked across to the girls' side on his first morning to chat with an old family friend over breakfast. It had been the talk of the school for days.

'It was a bit rubbish at the start,' Noah said, trying not to smile too much at the sensation of her hand folded in his. It felt good, a calming break. Normally he was a fidget, cracking his knuckles or picking his nails, particularly when he was concentrating. He hoped his fingers weren't clammy.

'You seemed quite happy to do your own thing. To be an individual rather than conform. The gregarious geek who could skateboard and hack into the school computer network. Who liked girls as friends, not just as dates. We hadn't seen that before.'

Anything to impress you, he thought. It was true, though. He had always had plenty of female friends to chirpse. In Clemmie's case, however, he was prepared to make an exception. And, if he was honest, the main reason he had agreed to move schools was because the girls there were so much fitter.

Noah knew, as they walked down the lane and past Curgurrell Farm Shop, that he should tell Clemmie about Alexei's letter; and her dad too. In his role as Home Secretary, Jack MacKenzie was in charge of MI5, the Security Service, and if there really was a mole within the British establishment, it was the job of MI5, not a fifteen-year-old boy, to uncover it. But then he remembered Alexei's words, his instruction to keep quiet until he had identified the mole. *I risk my life by telling you this, and you will risk yours if you tell others what you are doing. Do not go public on your spy website until you are certain of the mole's identity.*

His stomach tightened. For a brief moment he wondered if MacKenzie himself might be the mole. You couldn't get much more senior in the British establishment than Home Secretary. But it was a ridiculous thought and it disappeared as quickly as it had arrived. MacKenzie was a dyed-in-the-wool Conservative, more patriotic than anyone he had ever met, wasn't he?

'Shall we head back? Go for a swim in the pool?' Clemmie said, looking out to sea. The wind was ruffling her blonde hair and she was still holding his hand. Like her, he was old for his year and he had always been tall (gangly too, unfortunately); as she turned to face him, they were eye to eye, their heads close.

'That sounds good.'

Noah hadn't felt this happy for a long time. And then things got even better.

'And maybe we could go for a dip in the hot tub,' she added, giving him a peck on the lips. 'It was fun last time.'

4

NOAH STOOD BY reception, waiting for Clemmie to come down from her room with her swimming gear. The hotel foyer was still busy, the staff trying to remain courteous as Jack MacKenzie's ever expanding coterie of private secretaries, personal assistants, bag carriers and security guards swarmed around them, occasionally breaking off to talk too loudly into mobile phones.

'Can we just run through his requirements one more time?' a woman in a dark suit asked Julie, the hotel's long-term assistant manager, and Margaret, who was working on reception. Noah had got to know the staff by name over the years. They all knew who he was too, which had unnerved him when he was younger, but he now found it comforting, part of the ritual of the summer holiday, like the first sight of Carne Beach as they drove down the narrow, steep lane from Veryan.

He drew back into the shadows, standing in the corridor between reception and the lift, pretending to glance at the dinner menu displayed on a side table: hand-dived scallops with tempura cauliflower and belly of pork; prime Cornish fillet steak with Béarnaise sauce; crêpe Suzette. *You're going to Cornwall soon, no? To that smart hotel you're always telling me about? Where they set fire to their puddings?*

The thought of Alexei made him smile. He would enjoy it here – the quintessential Britishness of the place. Ironically, it was Barbara, the hotel's charming German maître d', who had the honour of soaking the crêpes in Grand Marnier and flambéing them, a duty she had performed with pyrotechnical aplomb for twenty years. His dad wasn't a big pudding man, but he always ordered crêpe Suzette at least once every holiday, just for the sheer spectacle of it. On a good day, the flames reached the restaurant ceiling.

'We need all the daily papers delivered to the Pendower Suite,' the woman was saying. Her manner was breezy, self-important. 'Every one of them.'

Noah edged a bit closer to hear the conversation, working his way along a series of framed *Vanity Fair* caricatures on the elaborately decorated wall, all tropical trees and birds. His mum, an artist, was always going on about the hotel's bespoke printed wallpaper – Lewis and Wood, apparently. He pretended to study the caricatures, each one signed 'SPY', which seemed to be a sign and gave him strength.

'Except the *Daily Sport*,' Julie corrected. Noah knew it wasn't the assistant manager's style to discuss guests' personal requirements so openly. She was the model of discretion, but the Home Secretary's party appeared to have set up permanent and very public camp in reception. 'He asked specifically for that not to be delivered last year.'

'Did he?' the woman said, surprised by Julie's efficiency. And maybe a little riled too, Noah thought.

'We've also ordered in a copy of *Superyacht World* magazine again,' Margaret added.

Noah felt his mouth go dry. Why would the Home Secretary want to read that?

'And he likes extra packets of the Cornish fairing biscuits,' Julie said. 'Sparkling water, not still, I believe, according to our notes.'

For a moment the woman in the suit was silent. Had she met

her match in Julie? Noah's mind was elsewhere, though. *Superyacht World*?

'Just don't give him any of that ghastly UHT stuff,' the woman said.

'No danger of that here, ma'am,' Julie replied, through what sounded like gritted teeth. 'We always put jugs of fresh milk in all the rooms.'

Noah glanced around him, keen to get away from reception and think through the implications of what he'd heard. He pressed the lift button just as the doors opened and Clemmie walked out, more gorgeous than ever.

'Are you alright?' she asked. 'You look like you've seen a ghost.'

'Feeling a bit peaky,' Noah mumbled. 'Might go and lie down in my room.'

He brushed past Clemmie, avoiding eye contact as he stepped into the lift, wishing the doors would close more quickly and speed him far away.

5

NOAH WALKED ALONG the corridor towards Room 15, trying to reassure himself that Jack MacKenzie's interest in superyachts was a coincidence. The Home Secretary liked Cornwall, liked being by the seaside, ergo he had an interest in all things maritime, including boats. Obvious, really. Not suspicious at all.

But it was no good. The hare of his imagination was up and running. Superyachts were niche, special interest, owned by the very few who could afford them, which was mainly Russian oligarchs, ones who needed to meet British traitors.

Another idea sailed into his thoughts. Was Clemmie involved too? Was she aware that he knew there was a mole in the British government? Was that why she was being so nice to him? Trying to throw him off the scent?

Stop, he told himself. *Please. Just stop.* Think of something nice. Afternoon tea in the drawing room. Fresh strawberry jam. Cool clotted cream.

Noah was too preoccupied to notice that his room door was ajar. He should have hung back, retreated to a safe distance and observed, but it was too late. He would have already been heard by whoever was inside. Cursing himself for dropping his guard, he paused and pushed open the door.

'Housekeeping,' a man in the middle of the room said with a

faint foreign accent. Noah hadn't seen him before. The uniform was right – white shirt, waistcoat, black trousers – but the tie was plain black. All male hotel staff wore Cornish hunting tartan ties, didn't they? 'Your main light was not working,' he added, gesturing towards the small chandelier in the middle of the room.

It was working this morning, Noah thought, but he said nothing and walked over to the window. 'Where are you from?' he asked. He liked the mix of nationalities amongst the hotel staff. It was what he enjoyed about his school too.

Small fishing boats were scattered across the bay. They were from Mevagissey, he assumed, in search of mackerel, maybe some pollock. 'Good pie fish,' his dad would always say when he returned from a fishing trip with too much pollock and nothing else.

'Romania,' the man replied.

Just like one of the waiters in the dining room, Noah thought, except that this man's accent sounded different. Was it more Russian? 'I hope you can continue to work here after Brexit,' he said.

'It should be fine,' the man replied. 'Maybe we will need visa.'

He was good, Noah thought, as he watched him leave the room clutching an old lightbulb. Well briefed. Just a shame about the tartan tie.

As soon as the door was closed, Noah pulled up a chair and examined the light fitting inside the chandelier. There was nothing obviously suspicious about it, but listening bugs could be tiny these days, as the staff in the Mayfair spy shops were always telling him.

After satisfying himself that the light was clean – it must have been a misdirection of some sort, a crude attempt to throw him off the scent – Noah set to work on the telephone handset, dismantling it quickly using a small penknife that he always carried with him (another present from his grandpa). Again, nothing obviously suspicious.

He did the same with the smoke alarm, which appeared untouched too; and the Roberts digital radio by his parents' bed, whose red leather panel he carefully unclipped from the back; and the Samsung HD box beside the TV, which was hidden in a large mahogany chest of drawers in the corner of the room. TV sets were always out of sight at the hotel – his favourite was in the library, where it was concealed, Blofeld-like, behind a moving panel of fake books, some of which were spy novels, natch.

Noah knew the situation called for a proper electronic sweep – 'technical surveillance counter-measures' or TSCM – but the latest equipment used by the professionals was way beyond his budget. At school, with help from his physics teacher, YouTube and eBay, he had managed to build his own spectrum analyser, using a software-defined radio, a TV tuner dongle, six AA batteries, a seven-inch LED screen and one open-source, single-board computer. It was a pretty basic piece of kit, no match for today's intelligence services, but they had swept the physics lab, picking up infrared transmissions from a TV remote.

Of course. Noah looked around the room and opened the chest of drawers again. He had forgotten to check the TV remote. Might it be transmitting more than was strictly necessary to change channels?

Five minutes later, the remote in pieces, he found what he was looking for: a tiny listening bug, no bigger than a petit pois, located next to its capacitors. Bingo. His first thought was to flush it down the loo or chuck it out the window. Instead, he dropped it into a glass of water and placed the glass in the bathroom for safekeeping.

6

'SORRY ABOUT EARLIER,' Noah said, walking around the poolside to where Clemmie was lying, sunning herself in a peach bikini as she read. 'Think I had a bit of sunstroke.'

'You looked terrible,' she replied, without raising her eyes from her book (*Me Before You*), which she was holding above her head with one hand, shielding her face from the sun.

Noah sat down on the lounger beside her, looking up as two blonde girls jumped into the pool. He recognised them as Cordy and Gee, the hotel proprietor's daughters. They were often around, mixing with guests' children, making people feel at home. Noah glanced across at Clemmie and saw that she had a navel piercing. Must be new, he thought. He only had himself to blame for her change of mood. The hot tub had been taken off the agenda for today, no question.

After finding the listening device in his TV remote, Noah had tried to get a grip, telling himself that he was imagining things. *Superyacht World* wasn't such a strange thing to read on holiday. It was aspirational, that's all; a wealthy Home Secretary looking ahead to his retirement. But the thoughts continued to tug at him like determined beggars.

'Is your dad into boats? Fancy big boats?' Noah asked after a few minutes, lying back on his lounger. He tried to make his question sound as casual as he could, as if there was nothing he cared less about in the world, but he knew it was a weird thing to ask.

'Not that I know of,' Clemmie said. 'Why?'

'Oh, nothing.' Noah clicked his knuckles. 'Just that your dad's people were in reception earlier, making sure that all the right things had been ordered for his room. Newspapers, magazines, that sort of thing.'

'And?'

'I overheard the receptionist saying your dad liked to read *Superyacht World* when he was staying here. And how they'd already got a copy in for him. Efficient or what?'

It was a few seconds before Clemmie spoke. Noah realised that he was holding his breath and told himself to relax.

'I know you like eavesdropping, pretending you're a spy,' she said, 'but I suggest you switch off for a bit, have a break from all that stuff. It's not good for you. And it's none of your business anyway, you nosy parker.' Then she added, 'At least it wasn't *Playboy*.'

'Sorry, you're right.' Noah wished he'd brought a book with him, something to busy himself with. Instead, he stared up at the cobalt-blue sky. 'It definitely wasn't *Playboy*. He didn't want the *Daily Sport* either. Although I wouldn't judge him if–'

'Noah, read a book.'

A pause. 'So he doesn't like superyachts, then?'

Silence.

'I've no idea. It's just something different to read on holiday, I guess. Something to take his mind off work. I bet you read strange things on holiday too. *Ham Radio Digest* or whatever.'

Wired, actually, but he said nothing.

7

AT 4 P.M. NOAH found himself sitting on the terrace, drinking Assam tea with his dad as they both smeared Rodda's clotted cream onto jam-laden scones. His grandpa was asleep next to them, snoring stertorously in the high afternoon sun, dressed in his dark-blue blazer and crimson cravat. Even asleep he looked distinguished, Noah thought. Moneyed, dapper, tough as old boots.

Clemmie was with her father, who had arrived amidst much fanfare. (His black ministerial car and an accompanying Range Rover had been parked facing uphill, 'ready for a quick getaway,' according to Sean, one of the hall porters.) His mum was having a swim and his dad hadn't demurred when Noah had asked if he wanted to join him for afternoon tea. It was a good sign, suggesting that he was unwinding, that they might be about to get on better.

There had always been the promise of closeness between them: a game of chess at the weekend; sitting in the car together in the school drive before being dropped off; his dad building a skateboard halfpipe in the garden for him. But it had never quite happened; common ground always seemed to elude them. A chess piece was invariably missing; evening chapel always beckoned; the halfpipe remained unfinished (the wrong wood), a soggy monument to what might have been.

'The MacKenzies are in town, I see,' his dad said, pouring them both another cup of tea. Despite living in London for twenty years, his dad's Glaswegian accent was strong, unlike Noah's, which was barely perceptible. He was lean and angular, like an overworked geography teacher, Noah always thought. And he had sported a trim beard for as long as Noah could remember. 'You still "friends" with the daughter?'

Noah's face reddened. 'It's nothing like that, Dad.'

'Did I say it was?'

They weren't angry with each other, though. At home, the conversation might have taken place at the end of the day, when they were both tired, and flared up like dry kindling. Noah would have stormed off to his bedroom, leaving his dad to shrug at his mum. Instead, now, in the summer sunshine, they just smiled at each other.

'Do you ever see him?' Noah asked. 'At work?'

'Who? MacKenzie? Our paths crossed a while back, when he was a junior minister.'

'Did you talk about Scotland?'

'He's Mr Big now. No time to sit around chatting to Weegies like me.'

Noah smiled, glancing around him. No one was close enough to overhear Dad's Glaswegian vernacular.

'How were the Lost Gardens of Heligan?' he asked. 'Did you find them?'

'They were good. Your mother's more interested in gardens than me, though.'

'Can I ask you something?'

'Sure.'

'When you first met Mum–'

'She didn't give me a second look.'

'Why not?'

'I was a shy fella from Glasgow, she was a posh Home Counties girl.'

Noah didn't see his mum as posh. He knew her father, his grandpa, was wealthy, having had a successful career in the City, and that they both spoke differently compared to his dad, but that was just because he was Scottish, wasn't it?

'And you were drawing a naked man?' Noah couldn't suppress a giggle. 'When you met?' He'd heard the story before, but it always made him laugh.

'It was an evening class. I was recently down from Glasgow, keen to expand my limited horizons. Thought I'd give life drawing a go. OK, so I wanted to find myself a lassie too.'

His dad had a habit of using Scottish words whenever he reminisced about his past. They would bubble up to the surface as if gasping for air. He had lost count of the number of times he'd cringed at being called a 'bairn' or a 'dafty' (although he secretly liked it). It was worse after he'd been watching Billy Connolly: 'Oot ma nut' had become a family catchphrase. Sometimes he wondered if his dad would have been happier staying in Glasgow and whether his life down south felt like a compromise.

'And you met Mum. Your future wifie.' Noah spoke the last word with an exaggerated Scottish accent, but his Dad didn't seem to notice.

'As I say, she was more interested in the male model than me.'

'How did you get her attention?'

'I made her laugh.'

'With your drawing?'

'I think she was curious. She'd led quite a sheltered life. Never met a Glaswegian before, let alone a fella from Partick.'

'If you had discovered something about Grandpa, something really bad, would that have changed your mind? Made you less keen on Mum?'

'Do you know something that I don't?' his dad joked, glancing at Noah's grandpa, who was still asleep.

'No!' Noah laughed, then became more serious. It was all coming out wrong. 'Not at all.' A part of Noah suddenly wanted to confess everything, share the burden of what Alexei had told him, but he knew he couldn't. Not yet.

'It's an interesting point,' his dad said. 'Sins of the father and all that. I think the sin itself is not passed down, but the consequences of it often are. Sometimes we have to live with our parents' mistakes, but we can't be blamed for them.'

'So if you fancy a girl but know something truly awful about the dad, it shouldn't put you off?'

'Jack MacKenzie is only a Conservative, Noah.' He laughed. 'Quite a long way to the right of the party, but he's not an axe murderer, as far as I'm aware.'

'Who said I was talking about Clemmie?' Noah said.

'Clemmie now, is it?' His dad broke open another scone and spread some more jam. 'She's a bonny girl. A bit out of your league, I'd have thought. Two years above, no?'

'One year.'

'Then go for it. Your mother's a year older than me.'

'We must both like older women.'

'Sins of the father.'

A moment later they were distracted by a commotion in the lounge. A uniformed policeman was calling a dog to heel, but the hound was more interested in Barbara, who was overseeing today's cream teas. Tail wagging like a demented windscreen wiper, the dog was bouncing around her.

'What's all that about?' Noah asked Julie, who'd walked over from another table of guests on the terrace to find out what was happening.

'Maybe the dog doesn't like Germans,' his grandpa muttered, woken from his slumber by the noise.

'Quite the opposite,' Julie said, watching as Barbara bent down to pet the dog. Julie seemed to have relaxed, satisfied that there was nothing to worry about. Noah knew that dogs were very welcome at the hotel, but they were generally discouraged from being in the sitting room when food – scones and cake in particular – was around.

'They seem very happy to see each other,' he said.

'And I think I know why,' his dad interjected. 'A sniffer dog, right? For the Home Secretary's visit?'

'He's called Oz,' Julie said, her usually unflappable voice cracking with emotion. 'The police asked the public for suggestions on Facebook and Twitter – once they knew he was a potential sniffer dog, they chose the name Oz in honour of Barbara's son, Olaf "Oz" Schmid, who was killed in Afghanistan trying to defuse an IED.'

Encouraged by Julie, Barbara brought the handsome German short-haired pointer outside onto the terrace, accompanied by his police handler, and introduced him to the group of dog-loving guests who had gathered round him.

Noah was aware from a previous visit that Barbara had lost a son, but he hadn't heard the details before. A staff sergeant with the 11 Explosive Ordnance Disposal Regiment Royal Logistic Corps, Olaf had been posthumously awarded the George Cross in 2010, Barbara explained in a cut-glass German accent. The George Cross was Britain's most prestigious gallantry award for 'bravery not in the face of the enemy'. After defusing more than seventy improvised explosive devices in Afghanistan, he was killed in Sangin the day before he was due to return to Britain.

'Olaf saved many soldiers' lives,' Barbara added, Oz now sitting at her feet, leaning into her legs. 'I am so happy they have named Oz after him. We first met when he was a puppy, and he always remembers me. I send him toys every month so he doesn't forget.'

The guests listened intently as she spoke. Noah noticed his grandpa had a tear in his tired, senescent eyes.

'And we're all safe now, are we?' a guest asked. 'Now that Oz has sniffed the Home Secretary's ministerial red boxes and swept the hotel?'

'All clear,' the policeman said, bending down to pat Oz. 'He's one of the best explosive search dogs I've ever worked with. Even has his own Twitter account, @TriForceOzzy, don't you boy?'

'More than can be said for me,' Noah's grandpa quipped.

'What's Tweeter?' another guest asked.

'And, of course, he follows @hotelhounds,' Julie said. 'Hector, Jenga and Izzy, the proprietor's dogs.'

But could Oz sniff out a traitor, Noah wondered? Did treachery have its own unique smell?

8

NOAH WALKED DOWN the road to Carne Beach where he stretched his legs, first one calf, then the other. The sun was still high, but the heat of the day was dissipating. It was cool enough for a quick run up to Nare Head. Noah wasn't one of the school's sports stars – not a member of the self-appointed social elite – but he was a quick runner and had worked out that he could stand on the wing in rugby (compulsory for boys) and keep out of harm's way. He'd also calculated the physics of place-kicking a rugby ball, a skill that had seen him rise through the teams, which hadn't been his intention at all.

His favourite sport was cross-country running (his father liked to run too, along the Thames footpath in his lunch-breaks, apparently), but the reason for today's jog was not fitness. It was a chance to order his thoughts.

Once he was up in the fields, above the beach, Noah began to lengthen his already considerable stride and see things more clearly as he followed the ridged track. It was essential, he now realised, to get himself out to Kreshensky's yacht as soon as possible and a plan to that end was already forming in his head. The hotel had recently acquired a thirty-eight-foot traditional gentleman's motor launch called *Alice Rose*, which was available for private charter or scheduled outings twice a week (Tuesdays and Saturdays). His dad had said on the drive down from London that he was keen to go out on it, possibly tomorrow, as they had a lunch planned with friends in St Mawes and his grandpa had announced that he wanted to arrive by water.

If Noah said he would like to go with them (which would either delight his parents or make them deeply suspicious), there might be an opportunity to set eyes on Kreshensky, or at least his yacht; a chance to get a feel for the enemy. More problematically, he needed to establish the oligarch's itinerary during his stay, try to second-guess where he might meet with his British mole. The butler was key to this, as Alexei said, but how could he find out which member of the hotel staff was his girlfriend? He couldn't go around asking each one of them. Way too embarrassing.

It all suddenly seemed beyond him and his limited teenage resources, but he had to try something, get on the front foot rather than wait for events to unfold.

Noah kept running along the coastpath, thinking things through. Kreshensky, as far as he could establish, had never visited the hotel in the past and there was no talk amongst the staff of his imminent arrival. (Noah had casually asked at reception.) And despite the Home Secretary's odd interest in superyachts, Noah couldn't assume that he was the mole, or that the mole was even a guest at the hotel.

As he crossed a small wooden footbridge in a deep gully below Nare Head, Noah became aware of two men up ahead, walking towards him down the steep path on the other side of the gully. Noah thought nothing of them at first, but he began to worry as he drew closer. Both men were thickset, one taller than the other. Neither was smiling and they weren't talking to each other. Instead, their cold gazes were fixed on Noah.

'Afternoon,' Noah offered as he ran past them at a fork in the path where another track led off to the right. He didn't like the looks on their faces, the way they glanced at each other just as he passed. A moment later, Noah felt their strong grip on both his arms as he was lifted in the air and frog-marched down the track to the right.

'Oi! Get off me!' he shouted, struggling to free himself. For a moment he resisted enough to halt their progress along the path, managing to trip up one of the men. He wasn't a great fighter – more sly than strong. A steep cliff, covered in bracken and grass, dropped down to the gully below, where a stream ran out to join the sea. It occurred to Noah that this wasn't a good place for a fight, or to lose your footing.

'What the hell are you doing?' Noah shouted again, as they tightened their grip and manhandled him down the track and into a deserted farm building that he'd seen from the main coastal path. There was no roof, just four stone walls and the remains of an old fireplace. He remembered his grandpa telling him that Dr Crippen, the notorious nineteenth-century murderer whose beheaded wife was found beneath the floorboards at their London house, was rumoured to have sought refuge in a hut below Nare Head. Was this the place? It wasn't a comforting thought.

They pushed him into the middle of the building so hard that Noah fell onto the mud floor and cut his head on a stone. When he looked up, one of the men, arms folded, was standing in the doorway. The other, the taller one, turned away, spun round and kicked Noah hard in the stomach as he lay on the ground. The pain was excruciating, like nothing he had ever felt before, not even when he had accidentally tackled the school's star winger in a house rugby match. (He'd been stretchered off the pitch a hero, but in truth he hadn't been able to get out of the way in time.) Was he going to die up here? No one could see them from the beach or the path.

'What is the meaning of this?' the man who had kicked him said.

Noah looked up at him, clutching his stomach. His head was starting to throb too.

The man was holding a small clear plastic bag. In it was the glass from his room, no longer with any water in it. The tiny listening bug, however, was still in the glass, which the man rattled. 'Who are you?'

Noah didn't reply. He didn't know what to say. Blood was trickling down his face now from the cut above his eye. He wiped it away. Should he tell them that he had once built his own spectrum analyser? That he knew about frequencies and covert transmitters, and had frankly expected better from the SVR, if that's who these people were? It had taken him barely ten minutes to locate and disable their listening bug.

The man kicked him hard in the stomach again. Noah groaned. He was in way too deep. He loved his country, Cornwall anyway, but not enough to die for it. Not at his age. He should forget everything that Alexei had told him at school, have a normal summer holiday like most teenagers. Drink a few beers and kiss some girls. Starting with Clemmie. In fact, just Clemmie. He didn't want to kiss anyone else. He didn't much like beer either, if he was honest.

'I was trying to change channels on my hotel TV,' Noah offered, knowing as soon as the words fell out of his mouth that they were feeble, not enough to save him. 'There was a problem with reception,' he continued, without any conviction now.

Another kick. This time Noah was braced for it and managed to shield his stomach from the worst of the impact.

'OK, OK, I'm a geek,' Noah cried out. 'I'm good at coding. Know all about Stuxnet. Nitro Zeus too. And, yes, I like physics – built my own spectrum analyser at school. Cost me fifty quid in parts on eBay, not including batteries. We used it to detect infrared transmissions from a TV remote in the lab. I took the remote in my hotel room apart for a bit of fun and found the bug, the one you've got there.'

The two men looked at each other. This time, his explanation seemed to have done the trick. No more kicks. They talked in

Russian for a few seconds, then the man who had kicked him spoke. 'Listen carefully, geeky boy. If you tell anyone about this…' He held up the bag with the listening device. 'Or us…' He glanced at his compatriot. 'We kill you. Understand?'

Noah nodded, but the men were already walking away, back down the track.

He lay on the muddy ground nursing his stomach. The pain was bearable, now that the men had gone. He was sure that they were SVR, Russia's foreign intelligence service. What had Alexei said? *Intelligence services are very protective – they prefer their moles to stay underground, away from daylight. I have no doubt our own SVR will be watching, listening.* Their presence here, the bug in his room, meant only one thing: the mole was staying at the hotel, or at least planning to visit at some point, perhaps to meet up with Kreshensky.

Noah wondered why he had been singled out. Had they bugged the whole hotel and decided to have a word with him after he had found and disabled the listening device in his room? It was the only explanation. The SVR were on site to ensure a smooth meeting between their handler and the British mole, whoever he was.

He struggled to his feet and fell over again, his legs shaking. He hadn't realised how much adrenaline was coursing through his torpid body. So much for the 'fight or flight' response. He hadn't fought and couldn't flee. He tried again, steadying himself against the stone walls of the building. He looked up and saw that the two men were high above him now, walking on the main coastpath towards Nare Head.

Across the bay, the hotel was gleaming in the sunshine. Further round, Portscatho, and there, off St Anthony Head, the profile of a yacht, Kreshensky's superyacht. Was it heading this way? Noah strained to look, wishing he had his binoculars with him. It was hard to tell. Either way, he knew now that he had to get himself on board.

9

NOAH WOULDN'T NORMALLY have accompanied his parents to the hotel's weekly Tuesday night cocktail party, but on this occasion he had accepted his dad's invitation to join them, as well as his offer of a tie. If he played his cards right, he could neck a glass of champagne when no one was looking. He needed one after his run.

A part of him hoped Clemmie would be there too, although it was going to be hard to act natural around her. He told himself the SVR were here to watch someone else, not her father, but there was no getting around the fact that Jack MacKenzie, Britain's Home Secretary, was now his number-one suspect. His heart sank. Just his luck to fall for the daughter of a national traitor. She would never forgive him for unmasking her dad.

Noah thought his parents looked in love tonight as they stood chatting in the Gallery, the room beside the Quarterdeck, admiring the colourful Terry Frost abstracts on the walls. His mum was more bohemian and less buttoned-up than his dad, all bright floral dresses and big ethnic necklaces. She loved to walk the coastpath and paint 'en plein air'. Noah liked to draw too – he found it calming. When he was younger, they would often paint together, particularly when he was bouncing off the walls. The moment he saw his mother get out the brushes, the world stilled and his buzzing brain began to quieten. Visits to the Tate Gallery at St Ives had a similar effect. It was where his mum had introduced him to Frost and the Newlyn School of Art. He liked to study the paintings and then turn to look out the gallery window at the sea and the surfers, whom he'd later be amongst. It made his world feel joined up, coherent.

The cocktail party had started on the dot of 7 p.m. and the room was filling up fast. Toby Ashworth, the hotel proprietor – navy-blue blazer, RNSA buttons, Royal Cornwall Yacht Club tie – introduced guests to one another and moved on, working the room, weaving people together in an effortless web of bonhomie. Noah watched as he stopped to chat with Daphne Burt, who had been a loyal part of the Ashworth family for more than sixty years. He had met her once, heard how she had played a crucial role in establishing the hotel after the family took it over in 1989.

Noah headed towards his parents, trying to listen in on other guests' conversations as he went. All around him staff poured Taittinger, the house champagne, and served canapés: smoked salmon, mackerel pate, crab tartlets. More guests arrived. Conversation flowed.

'Is it really true that this hotel is the largest quaffer of champagne in Cornwall?' he overheard someone ask a waiter.

'Allegedly, sir,' the waiter confirmed, topping up the man's glass.

Eavesdropping was a regular pastime for Noah, particularly in the dining room. One of his favourites from last summer was a retired judge talking to his recently divorced daughter. 'One has to put up with a few "untidinesses" in a long marriage,' he had chided. Untidinesses? What on earth did that mean, Noah had wondered.

'Can't wait to have our old dark-blue passports back again,' a wealthy farmer from Wiltshire announced, his sunburnt face matching the coral red of his corduroys. Noah recognised him from previous visits. He was hard to miss. 'They actually meant something in the world.'

'I find the French to be so very inefficient,' a doughty woman in pearls was saying to no one in particular. Noah assumed she was the farmer's wife. 'I mean, how many times over the years have we had to give France back to them?'

'Isn't May marvellous, though?' a tall woman said, beaming. She must have been beautiful once, Noah thought. She was still elegant, poised, her neck rising like a swan's from a grey merino top. 'And I like Merkel. Very straightforward, brave too. Not like all those men in Brussels. Jobs for the boys! Jobs for the Kinnocks!'

'What will that family do with themselves after Brexit?' the Wiltshire farmer asked.

'Interesting times ahead,' the woman in pearls said. 'Although I'm not sure I'll live to see them.'

'Some of them, dear,' the farmer consoled. 'Some of them.'

And then the Home Secretary entered, Clemmie on his arm. There was an audible lacuna, a pause in the hum of conversation, before the party continued.

These guests were a seasoned bunch, Noah thought – retired senior civil servants and top-ranking servicemen, captains of industry and High Court judges, people not easily seduced by the tawdry glamour of politicians, serving or otherwise. As Ken, the long-serving barman, had once put it to his dad, 'We have lots of ladies and sirs staying here, the odd dame too. They're landed gentry, you see, which makes all the difference.'

The Home Secretary was accompanied by two security guards, one of whom hovered by the door, the other following a few steps behind his charge. Clemmie caught Noah's eye, broke away from her father, who was now chatting to the hotel proprietor, and came over. She was wearing an off-the-shoulder scarlet evening dress and heels. Peng, Noah thought.

'What happened to your eye?' she said, sliding a glass of champagne off a passing waiter's tray.

Noah told her what he'd told his mother. 'I fell over on my run up to Nare Head.' Which was true. He just omitted to add that he'd been thrown to the ground by a Russian thug from the SVR.

'Ouch.'

'I'll live. Your dad's arrived, I see.'

'You noticed?'

A group of guests, mainly women, had gathered around the Home Secretary, who was holding forth on Brexit. He was a smooth operator, Noah thought – sharp light linen suit and tie, black hair slicked back, a winning smile – but he couldn't help thinking he was a bit too smooth. Sketchy. Some people called him oleaginous. His dad said that at least he'd done something else before entering politics, practising as a barrister in London after having read law at Edinburgh University. Private family wealth – his father was a substantial landowner in Sutherland – had facilitated both careers. Apparently he also excelled at shooting. Last year Noah had overheard a guest congratulating him on his recent 'left and right woodcock'.

'Was he driven down?' Noah asked.

'Train to Truro. His people picked him up at the station. Dad enjoys his trains. Like the Queen.'

'He didn't come by superyacht, then.'

Clemmie looked at Noah sideways.

'Sorry,' he said.

She raised her hand to his forehead, touching the wound lightly. 'Are you sure you shouldn't get someone to look at that?' Her hand dropped down, brushing his cheek on the way.

'It's fine.'

'I think we're the youngest guests here by a hundred and fifty years,' Clemmie whispered, looking around the room. 'Are your parents here?'

'Over there, discussing the pictures.'

'They seem happy.'

'They are, yes.'

'Love her dress. Mum would have enjoyed this sort of event – kept Dad's ego in check... and all those women at bay.'

Noah was aware that MacKenzie had become a bit of a pin-up for the Tory party.

'How long is it now? Three years?' he asked. Clemmie's mother had been French, a glamorous journalist who had fallen for a suave young Scottish politician. She'd been killed in a freak horse-riding accident.

Clemmie nodded and looked down. 'I miss her more every day.'

'I'm sure you do.' And now Noah had embarked on a train of events that might lead to Clemmie missing her father too.

Clemmie signalled for a top-up from a passing waiter, slipping her little finger into her glass as the champagne was poured.

'What's with the finger?' Noah asked as his own glass was refilled.

'An old trick Mum taught me,' she said, smiling. 'French women do it – the trace of hand cream on their finger diffuses the bubbles, which allows the glass to be filled to the top.' She raised her glass, which was fuller than Noah's. 'Santé.'

'Noah, isn't it?'

Noah turned to look at a man in his mid-forties who had joined them.

'So sorry,' the man said to Clemmie. 'I didn't mean to interrupt.'

'Not at all,' Clemmie replied, glancing at Noah for an explanation. He raised his eyebrows in confusion. She mouthed 'Laters' and walked over to join Cordy Ashworth, who was into ponies even more than Clemmie.

'Hope I didn't frighten her off,' the man said, his eyes lingering on Clemmie longer than Noah would have liked. He was wearing a plain brown jacket, graph-paper-patterned shirt and light chinos. Ex-army, Noah thought. Ginger hair, cut short at the back and sides, a trace of a harelip and a pale complexion that hadn't seen enough sun.

'She doesn't scare easily,' Noah said.

'So I gather. Shall we step outside?'

Sensing it was more of a polite instruction than a question, Noah followed the man through the open doors and out onto the terrace. The sky had darkened in the late afternoon, threatening rain, but it was still dry. They walked away from the guests who had spilled out from the Gallery.

'Wanted to have a quiet word,' the man said.

'What about?' Noah asked, but he already knew.

'I work for the British government, on the security side of things,' he began, drinking from his champagne glass. 'There's something you might be able to help us with.'

'Me?'

'I don't think it's a state secret that you are well versed in all things espionage. Your blog and so on. Your technical knowledge.'

Technical? Did this man know about the bug in his room too? If so, how? Had the British been listening in on the Russians? He should have left the bug where it was, not tried to show off by finding and disabling it.

'I'm not sure I follow you.'

'Nothing to worry about. Sometimes on holiday people see the strangest things, that's all. Unusual behaviour. Off-message. If you should happen to see anything, anything at all, give me a call, would you mind? Good to have another set of eyes and ears on the ground.' He paused. 'No need to mention our conversation to your parents. To anyone, actually.'

He handed Noah a card with a name – James Hilton – and a mobile phone number on it, before walking back inside to the party.

Noah studied the card and slipped it into his pocket. *Off-message.* Wasn't that how the media described aberrant politicians? Who was he? *I work for the British government, on the security side of things.* MI5, Noah assumed. Had he been tipped off about a possible mole? About MacKenzie? He looked out across the bay, the faint trace of boat wakes lying like gossamer on the still water.

So his website had been noticed by the 'powers that be', as Clemmie had suggested. This was what he wanted, wasn't it? The spy's life? He had just been told by someone calling himself James Hilton – so not his real name, obviously – to be an extra set of eyes and ears on the ground. It was exciting. He should be stoked, but he wasn't.

He returned to the Gallery and spotted his parents in the corner. They were with his grandpa, who was looking as spruce as ever, chatting to a couple whose backs were to him. His mum beckoned him over. As he approached, the couple they were talking to turned to greet him. He hadn't seen the woman before, but he recognised the man at once.

'This is our son, Noah,' his mum said. 'Meet Mr and Mrs Chapman. Peter and Anna.'

Noah froze. Two hours earlier 'Mr Chapman' had threatened to end his life.

'They're sailors, just arrived in Falmouth,' his dad added. 'On their way to the Scillies.'

And I'm Bob Marley's son, Noah thought, wincing at the memory of his earlier kicking. Peter Chapman smiled as he shook his hand.

'Pleasure to meet you,' he said, in a near perfect English accent.

'Have we met somewhere before?' Noah asked. He couldn't help himself.

'I don't think so,' Chapman said, fixing him with a stare.

'Noah hit his head this afternoon, fell over while out running,' his mum said, brushing back Noah's hair. Noah recoiled, not from teenage embarrassment, but because his wound still hurt.

'Sorry to hear that,' Chapman said. 'The coastpath can be a dangerous place.'

'Has anyone seen Clemmie?' Noah asked, desperate to get out of the room, which now felt hot and claustrophobic.

'I think I saw her by the pool,' his dad said.

'Thanks.' Noah nodded at everyone and walked away.

'Go carefully,' he heard the man call after him.

10

NOAH TOOK A loop around the pool even though he could see the loungers were all empty. He needed to walk. His stomach had been tight ever since he'd set eyes on 'Peter Chapman'. The man's English accent had been faultless, his manner unruffled. They might be lousy at hiding listening bugs, but the SVR knew how to carry off a cover story.

He was about to turn back and go to his room when he decided to check out the hot tub. It was through a set of double wooden doors at the far corner of the pool area. He approached with caution, remembering the story of how, one Christmas, a member of staff bearing two ordered glasses of Prosecco had apparently caught a couple *in flagrante delicto* in the hot tub. Noah had later discovered that it had in fact merely been a case of *in puris naturalibus* – one of several phrases he'd learnt in a banter-filled Latin class. Either way, he didn't want to find himself repeating the waiter's experience. He glanced around him and opened the doors.

'You took your time,' Clemmie said. She was in the bubbling water, head resting on her folded arms, staring out to sea. Noah couldn't say anything for a few seconds. He'd never seen her look so beautiful. 'Are you going to come in or just stand there like a lemon?' she asked.

'I'll go back and get my swimming trunks,' Noah said, turning to the door.

'Don't be such a prig.'

'What are you wearing, then?' he asked, curious. Clemmie, he noticed, had a tiny 'O' tattooed under her left arm.

'My swimsuit. Get in.'

'I've got my boxer shorts on.'

'I should hope so too. Hurry up, there's a draught.'

Noah closed the wooden doors, removed his jacket and trousers, his socks and lastly his shirt, leaving on his boxers. He then climbed in beside her and moved around, treading water.

'It's not a swimming pool,' she said. 'Relax.'

He moved to the front of the tub, next to Clemmie, and looked out at the glassy sea. In front of them was a solitary fishing boat, trapped in a pool of sudden late sunlight.

'Beautiful, isn't it?' she said.

'Can I tell you something?' he asked. 'Something secret?'

'Of course. We're not at school now.'

She was right: secrets had a habit of spreading quickly during term-time, ricocheting across social media like pinballs.

'You know Alexei,' he began, 'the Russian guy in my house?'

'The one you shared a room with?'

'Yeah. Well, his dad's in Putin's government.'

'I know. Let me guess: you think he and I should get it together, now that we both have famous dads in politics?'

'That's not what I was going to say.'

'That's a relief. I was getting a bit fed up with all the letters he kept writing to me.'

'Alexei?'

'Long – boring – billets-doux declaring his undying love for an English rose.'

'I had no idea.' He paused. 'He did once ask if it was OK to call a Scottish girl an English rose in a letter. I told him it was a bit of a thorny issue, but I think the joke was lost on him.'

'I can see why. He's given up now.'

'He once wrote me a letter too.'

'You as well?' she asked, eyebrows raised.

'Not that kind of letter. You aren't taking this very seriously.'

'Sorry.' She turned to face him in mock concentration, then hiccupped. 'I'm all yours.'

Noah wasn't sure how to proceed. Clemmie was in a weird mood. So was he.

'You know I'm into all this espionage stuff – run that website and everything.'

'You're a spy, Noah. Everyone knows that.'

'Well, I think Alexei told me something – in the letter – that's quite important.'

'He wants to defect?'

'Not exactly.'

Noah paused again, thinking through what he was about to say, which was unusual for him. He had a habit of blurting out thoughts before he'd considered them. There would be no going back once he'd told her. And he had no idea how she would react.

'Can I kiss you?' he asked. He wasn't proud of himself, his calculated opportunism, but it might be the last chance he ever got for a snog with Clemmie MacKenzie.

She didn't say anything. Instead, she leant forward and gave him a long, slow, lingering kiss that he hoped would never end.

'Better now?' she said, stroking his hair. 'You really should get that cut looked at.'

'Going back to Alexei…' he said, his brain whirring.

'If we must.'

'He told me that there's a traitor in the British establishment, very high up. Someone who's working for Putin – a mole.'

'Your spying obsession must be contagious.'

'I think this person – this mole – might be staying right here, at the hotel.'

'Doesn't surprise me. The hotel's full of establishment types.

They're all pretty patriotic, though. And most of them are retired.'

'Not all of them.' He took a deep breath, studying Clemmie's profile as she stared out to sea. 'Your dad isn't, for example.'

There was a pause, the moment that Noah had been dreading. It wouldn't have come as a surprise if Clemmie had slapped him hard in the face, climbed out of the hot tub and walked off. Instead, she laughed, a dry, uncommitted laugh, and then turned to Noah.

'You're not serious, are you?' she asked. Noah looked away. 'Oh God, you are serious.'

'The mole has a handler,' he continued. 'That's how these things work. And in this case, I think the handler might be someone called Oleg Kreshensky, a Russian oligarch, the one who's just arrived in Falmouth.' He paused. 'On a superyacht.'

'Which is why you asked about the magazine.'

'I'm sorry, Clemmie. I'm sure there's an innocent explanation.'

She turned away, a sadness spreading across her face. It wasn't how Noah had expected her to react. 'How did Alexei know?' she asked quietly. 'About the mole?'

'He overheard his dad at a dinner party back home in Moscow.'

'And he told you?'

'He's trying to help his dad. He's a secret renegade, apparently, one of a growing number of ministers who are against Putin and want the West to help unseat him. Alexei hasn't told his dad, but he thought I could help him if I unmasked the mole on my website.'

'He's the Home Secretary, Noah. You've seen him on TV. He's as loyal as they get. Pro-Brexit, hard on immigration, tough on crime.'

'I know all that. Which is why I honestly don't think it's him. I just wanted to tell you. Share it with someone.'

Another silence, longer this time.

'The funny thing is,' Clemmie said, turning to face him, 'it could be Dad.'

'How do you mean?'

'I hardly know him, if I'm honest. He's always busy, never comes to school any more, works during the holidays, is more interested in his ministerial red boxes than my school reports. What I do know is that he's not been himself recently. Been behaving strangely.'

Off-message. 'Like what?'

'Even I was surprised by the magazine when you told me.'

'Really?'

'He's taken up running too. Started back in the Easter holidays. Not like him at all. Early-morning jogs around Green Park. One day he didn't tell his security guards. Slipped out the back door. They were furious with him. He told me over breakfast that he just wanted a break from all the attention, a few minutes to himself. But he loves all that, all this.' She nodded in the direction of the drinks party.

'Will you help me? Clear his name. Get him out of the picture so we can find the real mole?'

'Be Bond's sidekick, you mean.'

'My Felix Leiter.'

'Sure.'

'It won't be easy. The Russians are in town. And MI5.'

'How do you know all this?'

Noah proceeded to tell her about finding the bug in the room and how he'd been beaten up by two SVR officers on his run – the real reason for the cut on his head. He mentioned James Hilton, the MI5 officer too.

'Are you still interested?' he asked. Clemmie nodded. 'Then meet me at reception after breakfast tomorrow.'

'Where are we going?'

'On a boat trip.'

11

CLEMMIE AND NOAH stood by the lift, waiting for it to arrive from the basement. They had changed back into their clothes after the hot tub. Noah had discreetly removed his wet boxer shorts while he was drying himself with a towel, wrung them out and now had them clutched tightly in one hand. He hoped no one would notice.

The lift door opened and the Russian man, 'Peter Chapman', was standing there. Odd, Noah thought. No swimming trunks or sports kit. The only reason to visit the basement was to use the swimming pool or the gym.

'Good evening, Noah,' the Russian said in perfect English, without missing a beat. He acknowledged Clemmie with a smile and moved back to make room for them.

The lift ascended in silence. Noah stared at the control panel: 'Five Persons, 375 kg'. That's seventy-five kilogrammes per person, he thought. Who calculated such things? He glanced across at Clemmie, who looked back at him, then up at the wound on his forehead. He hoped she wouldn't say anything about it now. He clicked his knuckles, which did nothing to release the tension.

The doors opened and the Russian gestured to let Noah and Clemmie out first before turning right to walk down the corridor. He was unusually silent, Noah thought; no loaded comments.

'Are you in the Pendower Suite too?' Noah asked Clemmie once the man had gone.

She leant forward, her mouth close to his ear. 'We're not actually staying in the Pendower,' she whispered, suppressing a giggle. 'Late room switch – for security reasons. We're now in the Kiberick Suite.' She gestured at the door behind her. 'And get this: it's actually Room 20, but our wooden key fob has "21" on it.'

'That should fox them,' he whispered back.

'Security are in 19 – there's an adjoining door. And I've got my very own cute "cabin room".'

'Me too. I'm going back down in the lift again.'

'Why?'

'That was the man who beat me up,' Noah said, nodding down the corridor where the Russian had gone.

'Him? But he was English.'

'That's why I'll make a good spy and you won't,' Noah said as the lift doors opened again. 'He was at the cocktail party earlier, talking to my parents in perfect English, as if nothing had ever happened.'

'Where are you going?'

'To the basement. Chapman came up from there in a suit. No sign of having been for a swim or used the gym. Don't you think that's a bit odd?'

Noah stepped into the lift, smiling at Clemmie as the doors started to close. At the last moment she jumped through the gap and almost fell into his arms. She gave him another kiss. 'You're good at this, aren't you?'

He didn't know if she meant kissing or spying. The lift descended past the ground floor and kept on going to the basement. Noah went first, glancing at the rude Gerald Scarfe caricatures on the walls. He smiled as he remembered asking his dad when he was younger what they were all about. That was before he'd discovered the salacious Aubrey Beardsley pictures down by the Carne Suite, beyond where Clemmie was staying, which had been an education. But even they seemed tame compared to the Roger Hilton 'The Party' picture in the gents loo...

'In this one,' Noah said, pointing at a caricature above a basket where people left their swimming towels, 'he really is talking out of his–'

'What are you doing?' Clemmie asked as Noah picked up a chair and took it back over to the lift. He swung open the outer door and placed the chair between the inner sliding doors to prevent them from closing.

'I just want to see what he was doing here, that's all. And I don't want him coming back down.'

The gym, which overlooked the pool, was empty, the exercise machines standing silent. Noah could never understand why people might want to use a running machine when the coastal paths beckoned. He glanced through the windows at the pool, which was illuminated by underwater lighting. There didn't seem to be anyone in it, or in the adjacent whirlpool.

He opened the door into the pool area and stopped in his tracks. A faint glow was emanating from the sauna room ahead. A bad feeling too. He could just make out the profile of a man through the smoked-glass door, sitting upright on the slatted wooden bench and staring ahead. Noah swallowed hard and reached for Clemmie's hand. The man was too still.

'Is someone in there?' Clemmie asked, now at his shoulder, her voice a whisper.

'Go back into the other room,' he said and stepped forward. He waited for Clemmie to leave, opened the glass door and was hit by a wall of heat.

'Everything alright, sir?'

Noah spun round to see Andrew, one of the concierges, who had emerged behind them. How had he got down here? There had to be another way to access the basement, Noah thought.

'Staff stairs,' Andrew said, reading Noah's confusion. 'The lift wasn't working.' He looked back at Noah and then at the sauna, his usually smiling face etched with concern. 'We've got a light behind reception – tells us how long the sauna's been on for. To stop the risk of fire. It's been on for a long while, so I came down to take a–'

'I think he's dead,' Noah said quietly, gesturing at the figure beyond the glass door, which he had closed.

'Dear God,' Andrew whispered, crossing himself as he stepped forward. All three of them stood there in silence before Andrew spoke again. 'You two better go upstairs.'

12

NOAH COULDN'T SLEEP that night, his teenage brain buzzing more than usual. After they had discovered the body, he and Clemmie had gone straight to reception and explained that there was a dead man in the sauna room. Andrew had already rung through to tell them. Noah didn't know what name the guest had used to check into the hotel, but he suggested the person might be someone called James Hilton, whom he'd met at the cocktail party earlier.

The police were summoned, along with the local GP and undertaker, and the body was removed with discretion and respect via the staff stairs and out through the tradesman's entrance. It was assumed amongst the staff that the man had had a heart attack, particularly given that statins, aspirins and beta-blockers were found in his room. Deaths at the hotel were very rare but not unprecedented, and Noah knew, from all his eavesdropping, that they didn't necessarily involve elderly guests. On one occasion a few years ago, the resident pianist had apparently fallen off his stool stone dead in front of all the guests in the dining room while playing a number from *My Fair Lady*. The head waiter, wearing tails, had promptly commandeered two commis waiters to give the pianist a hero's chairlift out of the room, explaining to guests that he had merely fainted. After twenty minutes of valiant CPR behind the scenes, an ambulance had arrived and he had been pronounced dead from a heart attack.

No guests seemed to be aware of James Hilton's demise, except for the Home Secretary's party who were informed as a matter of courtesy. Noah had no proof, of course, but he feared that 'Peter Chapman', the Russian, was responsible, the sauna death being part of a new turf war between the SVR and MI5. Weren't spies meant to be more nuanced in their rivalries, fighting cold wars in the shadows? As he had said to Clemmie, this was more like Cluedo, where people were felled by lead piping in the library.

Sleep was finally ensnaring Noah when his phone vibrated. It was Clemmie on WhatsApp.

'You awake?' she had typed.

'Almost.'

'Sorry. Just so awful.'

'I know.'

'That could have been you – on your run.'

'Don't remind me.'

They chatted some more, each keen to unburden themselves of the weight of the evening's events. Noah tried to imagine Clemmie lying in her cabin room as he lay in his. It sounded about the same size: small, cosy, intimate. He wished he was with her now, snuggled up together, comforting each other.

It was the man's open eyes that had got to Noah. That and the heat inside the sauna. Any DNA evidence would have been swiftly destroyed at that temperature. It reminded him of Gareth Williams, the GCHQ employee who had been found dead in a padlocked North Face holdall a few years earlier in Pimlico. His flat's heating had been turned up to maximum to hasten the deterioration of the body.

He and Clemmie had agreed to tell no one, least of all her dad, about his theory that James Hilton had been killed by the Russians. But MacKenzie's people had anyway enforced a lockdown on all the rooms occupied by the Home Secretary's party, including Clemmie's. It wasn't clear if that was on account of the death or because of something else that had spooked his security.

Noah was beginning to think that she had fallen asleep when another message appeared on WhatsApp.

'Could be Dad.'

'?' Noah typed.

'Mole.'

'Why?'

'He went AWOL again this afternoon. Security found him walking on Pendower Beach. No phone, nothing. Just walking. Odd.'

'Sure there's an innocent explanation.'

Noah just wished he knew what it was.

13

Noah's parents were surprised when he joined them and his grandpa for breakfast at a corner table in the sunlit dining room at 8 a.m. They were even more surprised when he announced that he'd like to come with them on *Alice Rose* to St Mawes, where they were due to have lunch with some old friends who lived near the castle.

'And if it's OK, I'd like to bring Clemmie along too,' he said. 'Maybe when you go to your lunch, we could stay on board the boat, go for a little cruise. Across to Falmouth, perhaps.'

'Third-largest natural deep-water harbour in the world,' his grandpa declared, as if for the first time. 'Rio, Sydney, Falmouth.'

Noah's parents exchanged looks. Noah glanced at his grandpa, who winked at him.

'I don't see why not,' his dad said. 'You could take a packed lunch. I'm sure the hotel will prepare one for you.'

As they chatted, it became apparent that his parents were unaware that a hotel guest had died the previous night, let alone that Noah had discovered the body. He saw no reason to say anything – it would only upset them, particularly his mum. If the morning staff knew, they weren't letting on either. Ditto the other guests. It was business as usual.

'Darling, are you sure your head's OK today?' his mum said. 'It looks very bruised.'

'Come up quite a shiner,' his grandpa added, almost approvingly, 'for an innocent fall.' Had he suspected the real reason for the wound? It wouldn't have surprised Noah.

'I'm fine, Mum,' Noah said. A moment later he felt anything but fine as 'Peter Chapman', the Russian who had kicked seven bells out of him on the coastpath, walked past with his wife, 'Anna'.

'Good morning,' he said, his gaze lingering on Noah as they stopped to chat to his parents.

Noah had woken up that morning feeling different about 'James Hilton' and the cause of his death in the sauna. He had been too quick to blame the Russian, too conspiratorialist. It could have been a heart attack, given the medication found in his room. Now, though, as he looked at the Russian, the old storm clouds of suspicion came rolling back in, darkening his world. An image of Chapman in Hilton's room, leaving the heart medication beside the bed, flashed in his mind like lightning.

While Noah's parents made polite conversation, his grandpa read the newspaper and spooned thick home-made marmalade onto his toast. He liked to check the share prices first, then return to the news, reading out amusing titbits to anyone who would listen. He finished up with the obituaries and death announcements, scanning for familiar names, though he had already outlived most of his friends.

'He's a wrong'un, that one,' he whispered to Noah when Peter Chapman and his wife finally moved on to their own table.

'How do you mean?' Noah asked, but his grandpa chose not to hear, as he often did these days.

'Ah, our favourite member of staff.' His grandpa looked up and beamed.

'Good morning,' the approaching waitress said. 'And how is everyone today?'

'Better for seeing you, Rita,' his grandpa said. Noah squirmed as he caught the young blonde waitress's eye, but she didn't seem to mind the flattery. At least his grandpa hadn't told her that she was looking winsome, as he often did.

'Assam tea for you both, ma'am?' she asked his parents in a faintly Eastern European accent. 'And Earl Grey for you, sir?' she added, turning to his grandpa.

'Thank you, my dear,' he purred. 'And you know already what I'll be having to eat.'

'Smoked haddock, poached egg on side, two slices of brown toast?'

'You've got it,' he said. Then he paused and turned to Noah. 'Or is today a kipper day, I wonder?'

Noah smiled. It was his grandpa who had first introduced him to the hotel's kippers, waxing lyrical about their lightly smoked, fleshy meat. He was more of a bacon-and-black-pudding man himself.

'And, please, don't forget the powdered ginger,' Rita added. Every year she would pass on health tips to his grandpa, not that he needed them. 'When you have the sore throat, or feeling cold, one tablespoon of ginger, mixed with honey, boosts immune system. This is also good for gut.'

She took the others' orders and was about to return to the kitchen when Noah's dad stopped her.

'Rita, I don't suppose you know if it's too late to order lunch – for two – on *Alice Rose* today?'

'Sir, I believe you will find full lunch and drinks are provided anyway.'

'The three of us are going over to St Mawes for a bite to eat, but Noah here will stay on board with a pal. They might take a spin over to Falmouth, maybe up the Helford, and you know what teenagers are like – always starving,' he added, glancing at Noah.

Noah noticed a fleeting smile pass across the waitress's face, an almost imperceptible lightening of her features.

'There is a big boat there right now,' she said. 'A superyacht.'

'So I gather,' his dad said. 'I read something in the local paper.'

'Have you been to see it yourself?' Noah asked. 'Had a look at it?' He wasn't one to chat up the waitresses – that was his grandpa's job – but something made him want to continue the conversation.

'I would like this very much, but we are too busy at the moment.' She paused. 'I have one friend, a Russian. He lives in Gavri, just five kilometres inside Russia. My family cross the border often to buy sugar and wholegrains. Prices are much cheaper than in Latvia. He is here in Cornwall now – he arrived yesterday on this big boat.'

'Doing what?' Noah asked, but he knew exactly what her friend was doing.

'Being butler.'

Noah struggled to maintain his composure; his mouth had gone dry. He could feel his parents' eyes on him. They would be puzzled by his early-morning loquaciousness.

'The owner is Russian,' Rita continued. 'Very rich man. And horrible boss,' she added, laughing, looking around her. 'Not like here.'

'In what way?' Noah continued. He couldn't help himself now; he no longer cared. 'How is he horrible?'

'Every year I want to see my friend. He comes last year to Falmouth too. But he is not allowed to take time off. He must always stay on the boat. It is very frustrating.'

'I think we must let Rita get on with her job,' his dad interrupted. 'Other people are waiting for their breakfasts.'

'Right,' Noah said, trying to focus, but he was already behind the wheel of *Alice Rose*, speeding towards a superyacht with a plan for how to get himself on board.

14

Noah was waiting for the lift when the waitress from yesterday, the one studying forensic science, walked past.

'Hi there,' he said. He had been hoping to see her today.

'Good morning, Noah,' she said. Another one who had learnt his name.

'Can we have a quick chat?' he asked. 'In private.'

She blushed and glanced to left and right.

'About last night,' Noah added, hoping to avoid any misunderstanding, but managing to create more. He was blushing himself now. 'The guest, Mr Hilton.'

Her eyes seemed to light up.

'It was you who found the body, wasn't it?' she asked, sotto voce.

Noah nodded. 'Have you got a second?' The lift doors opened. 'I just want to show you something. Ask your advice.'

Downstairs in the basement, the waitress, who introduced herself as Sophie, explained to Noah that she'd heard about the death first thing that morning as soon as she'd arrived. The staff were talking about nothing else, but not with the guests.

'The police and the doctor are saying it was a heart attack,' Noah said, opening the door to the swimming pool area. For a second he flinched, remembering the outline of the figure in the sauna the night before. 'I was just wondering what you thought, given your studies at uni?'

'How do you mean?' Sophie asked.

He was hoping that she might be sufficiently intrigued by a real-life crime scene to help him. 'Are there any signs that it could have been something else?' he asked. 'Not a heart attack?'

'Why are you so interested?'

'Just curious. Thought you might be too. I met Mr Hilton at last night's drinks party, a few hours before he died. Seemed like a nice bloke. Not the sort about to keel over and die.'

Sophie eyed him for a moment.

'It hasn't been sealed as a crime scene, so it's hard to tell,' she said, opening the sauna's glass door. 'I'm meant to be on duty upstairs.'

Noah stood back as she bent down in the sauna to look at the slatted wooden seat, the walls, the inside of the door.

'What are you searching for?'

'Blood. If there are any traces, I could take a sample, put it in a phial and test it. See if it's human. I've got a small crime-scene kit in my room,' she added. 'We're meant to practise with them in the holidays.'

'Perfect,' Noah said, noticing that Sophie had stopped moving around in the sauna and was focusing on the seat. 'Found anything?'

'There might be something under the slat here,' she said, her tone more serious now.

Noah tensed. 'Blood?'

'Hard to tell. Could be anything. I need to come back with my kit. The moisture in the room might be a problem. Blood dries from the outside in, so if it leaves a ring when you wipe it, you can get an idea how long it's been there for. And if the drop's arrived from an angle, that can also tell you how it got there.'

She'd make a good forensics officer, Noah thought. Professional, unruffled.

'Let me know if you find anything,' he said.

'I'll need to tell the police if I do.'

15

NOAH STOOD ON the jetty beside Smugglers' Cottage at Tolverne, on the River Fal, just north of the King Harry chain ferry. It was a beautiful, fertile stretch of the river, he thought, the banks cloaked in sessile oaks, their branches hovering over the water's edge at the high-tide mark. He had been driven from the hotel by Sean, the porter, who was now loading victuals on board *Alice Rose* with Rita, who had revealed during the fifteen-minute car journey that she had studied hospitality management at Riga University.

It turned out that she could also speak Russian – it was the second most common language in Latvia, she explained, a legacy from its years as a member of the Soviet Union. Handy, too, if you had a Russian boyfriend, Noah thought. He had asked at reception if Rita could accompany them on *Alice Rose*, realising that she was his ticket to get aboard the superyacht. It was a timely request. The launch was normally crewed by husband-and-wife team Simon and Susie, but Susie was away today, looking after her kitchen-design business, so Rita was a welcome replacement.

Before they'd left the hotel, Noah had explained to Rita that they might take a look at the Russian superyacht after dropping his parents off at St Mawes. Her eyes had lit up when he'd suggested that she text her Russian friend. He hadn't asked if this friend could get him on board *The White* – that would have to wait. She loved everything connected with water, she'd told him in the car. Latgale, the region she was from, was known as 'blue-lake land', apparently, and her dream was to live and work beside the Mediterranean. Cornwall wasn't quite the Med, but on a day like today – aquamarine sea, cloudless skies – it could give it a good run for its money, Noah thought.

Simon, the coxswain, was already on board *Alice Rose*, which was moored at the end of a long pontoon. She was a good-looking launch, Noah thought, as they all walked down towards her. Classic sweeping lines and a cedar-wood hull with teak decking, according to Sean, who had described it to them in the car. Apparently she was capable of twenty-four knots and had been built in 2008 by Cockwell's, a firm of local boatbuilders who worked out of a traditional yard a few miles away in Mylor Creek.

'This place is brimming with history, you know,' Noah's grandpa said, looking up and down the river. 'It was right here that General Eisenhower briefed his American troops from the 29th Infantry Division before they embarked for their D-Day landings on Omaha Beach in 1944. Twenty-seven thousand of them in the Fal Estuary – I can see them now, mustering on the shoreline. The general stayed up there, in Smuggler's Cottage.'

Noah glanced behind him as they reached *Alice Rose*, trying to picture the scene. His grandpa was always dropping in little nuggets of history into conversation. If only his GCSE history lessons were as interesting.

Simon welcomed them with warmth and efficiency, running through a safety drill on the pontoon before they boarded. He told them he'd served in the army for more than thirty years, but he slipped *Alice Rose*'s moorings with all the skill of a navy man. He struck Noah as an eminently sensible coxswain: rugged, thorough and just the sort of man you'd want beside you in a crisis.

His grandpa joined Simon at the wheel, looking at the navigation screens, while Noah's parents settled down in the stern, enjoying the sunshine and the wind in their hair. Noah and Clemmie sat down next to them as Rita busied herself below decks, rustling up coffee and home-made biscuits for everyone.

Alice Rose made her way down the river, past half-hidden creeks. They looked enticing, Noah thought; good places to hide. In the middle of the river was a row of floating mussel beds, the shells growing on ropes beneath the water.

'You OK?' he asked, turning to Clemmie, who had been quiet for a while.

'I'm always sick on boats,' she said.

'You won't be on this one,' Simon interjected. 'Smooth as they come.'

'Fix your gaze on the horizon,' Noah said, making room for his grandpa, who had come back to sit with them. Noah was amazed at how agile he still was.

'Good shoes for a boat,' his grandpa said, nodding at Noah's Doc Martens. 'Rubber soles, very quiet.'

'Incoming St Nazaire story,' his dad whispered as he shuffled along the stern seat.

'What was that?' his grandpa asked.

'Nothing.'

'Have I told you about the raid on St Nazaire?' he continued.

Noah's dad shook his head at him, as if to indicate that he hadn't.

'No, Grandpa,' Noah said, 'I don't think you have.' And then, in a whisper to Clemmie, 'You should hear this – he's full of cool war stories.'

Clemmie didn't look that keen, but she was far too polite not to listen.

For the next five minutes, his grandpa told them all about Operation Chariot, the daring raid in 1942 on the port of St Nazaire in Brittany that he'd participated in. At the time, the

German battleship *Tirpitz* was posing a grave threat to the Atlantic convoys. It was a huge vessel and the German-held dry dock at St Nazaire was the only place in Europe that was big enough for it to be serviced. So an audacious plan was hatched to destroy the dock by ramming it with an obsolete British destroyer, HMS *Campbeltown*, that had been packed with explosives.

'On 26 March 1942, HMS *Campbeltown* left Falmouth accompanied by a flotilla of sixteen launches, plus several torpedo boats and gunboats, and a fighting force of six hundred and eleven British sailors and commandos,' his grandpa said with the authority of someone who had told the story many times. 'Two Hunt-class destroyers escorted us.

'The *Campbeltown* managed to get within a mile of the dock, flashing genuine German recognition signals, before they opened fire on her. On the final approach, the skeleton crew took down the flag of the Kriegsmarine and hoisted the fighting ensign of the Royal Navy. The commandos, meanwhile, set about blowing up as much of the dock's equipment and machinery as they could.

'And we wore soft soles, just like yours,' his grandpa added, nodding at Noah's Doc Martens, 'to help us run around the docks undetected. And do you know what our agreed code word was, so that we didn't shoot each other in the dark?'

'Tell us, Grandpa,' Noah said, turning to Clemmie, who seemed to have overcome her seasickness and was now entranced by the story and its teller.

'Wee Willie Winkie.' He beamed. 'Because the Germans couldn't pronounce their Ws!'

They all fell about laughing, Noah remembering now that he had heard the story before, a long time ago, maybe several times. There were 169 British casualties, a further 215 were captured and 222 escaped by small craft back to Britain, including his grandpa. Incredibly, five escaped through France and made their way down to Gibraltar and then back to the UK.

'The Germans searched the *Campbeltown* but didn't find anything,' his grandpa continued. 'Twenty-four depth charges – four tonnes of high explosive! – had been hidden in sealed steel tanks below the forward gun. They blew up at noon the following day, more than ten hours after the *Campbeltown* had rammed the dock gates. Two hundred and fifty German soldiers and French civilians were killed, and the dry dock was destroyed.

'It was unusable for the rest of the war – I don't think it was finally repaired until 1947. Two days later, there was another huge explosion, caused by delayed-action torpedoes that had been fired into the outer dock gates. Panic ensued and many local French civilians were shot after being suspected, unfairly, of involvement in the raid.'

'What he won't tell you is that five people received the Victoria Cross, the highest number for a single wartime action, and more than eighty others were decorated,' Noah's dad said, smiling at his grandpa, 'including yours truly here.'

'It was the greatest raid of all,' his grandpa concluded, sitting back, his eyes moistening.

'And it started from just over there,' Simon added, looking across to Falmouth Harbour.

A respectful silence fell on the boat.

'I think I might be wearing the wrong shoes,' Clemmie whispered, glancing at her wedge-heeled espadrilles.

16

NOAH WASN'T LOOKING at Falmouth Harbour. His eyes were on the ninety-metre superyacht that was anchored offshore. It was the closest he had been to *The White* and the sheer scale of the glossy vessel took his breath away, its multiple decks layered like a wedding cake.

'Twenty-six crew, cruising speed of fifteen knots,' Simon said, noticing where Noah was looking. 'A beauty, isn't she? Comes here every year on her way from the Scillies to the Scottish Highlands. And every four years, she gets a refit at the Pendennis Shipyard in Falmouth.'

'Do you know who owns it?' Clemmie asked him. Noah glanced at her, surprised by the question. He'd told her to act as if she knew nothing about Kreshensky. For a moment he wondered if it had been a mistake to confide in her. Had she mentioned anything to her father?

'Some Russian oligarch,' Simon said.

'Rita knows him,' Noah said, glancing at the waitress, keen to take control of the conversation. 'Don't you, Rita?'

'I don't *know* him.' She laughed. 'I just know he is very mean man.'

'That's why he's so rich,' Simon quipped.

'Rita's got a friend who works on the yacht,' Noah said. Rita blushed. 'We thought we might take a closer look after we've dropped off the others in St Mawes.'

'Sounds good to me,' Simon said, glancing at Noah's parents, who were more interested in the *Duchess of Cornwall*, one of the ferries that operated between St Mawes and Falmouth. His grandpa waved at the ferry's passengers as it passed them 'port to port'.

Five minutes later, his parents and grandpa were safely ashore and Simon was steering *Alice Rose* out of St Mawes Harbour, the town's small Henry VIII castle to starboard. It was just Noah, Rita, Clemmie and Simon on board now.

'So, where do you two young lovebirds want to go?' Simon asked, throttling back as he left St Mawes behind. 'Find a nice mooring up the Helford for lunch? Or take a butcher's at the Russian boat first?'

Noah looked at Clemmie and then at Rita. He knew what he wanted to do, but Simon had other ideas.

'There's an interesting place near Port Navas, on the north shore of the Helford,' he continued. 'A big house called Ridifarne.'

'Sounds familiar,' Noah said. 'I think Grandpa might have mentioned it once.'

Clemmie shuffled next to him, sensing another incoming war story, Noah thought.

'A unit of the Special Operations Executive was based there during the war,' Simon continued. 'They used it to launch various raids on Brittany, liaising with the French Resistance and ferrying SOE agents back and forth in a flotilla of Breton fishing boats. One of the vessels, *L'Angèle-Rouge*, had a small engine for fishing, but it also had two other secret engines that could take it up to twenty knots – as fast as *Alice Rose*. Incredible. I'm sure your grandfather knows all about it.'

'He's definitely mentioned the SOE on the Helford,' Noah said, remembering a story his grandpa had told him about special 'surf-boats' fitted with Bren guns. 'Didn't they rescue British pilots off the beach, ones that had been shot down over France?'

'That's them.'

'I'd love to see the place,' he said, trying to sound diplomatic, 'but maybe another time?' He glanced at Clemmie. Right now the only thing on his mind was getting aboard *The White*. 'Perhaps we can look at the yacht now?'

'Fine by me,' Simon said. 'Does your friend know we're coming, Rita? Sometimes these superyachts aren't so keen on other boats getting too close.'

'I'll text him again,' Rita said.

The reality of what lay ahead began to dawn on Noah as they crossed Carrick Roads – the local name for the Fal Estuary, according to Simon, derived from the Cornish for 'rock anchorage' – and drew near to *The White*, close enough to read its name written in extravagant italics on the hull. The vast ship looked otherworldly in its shininess.

There were no obvious signs of activity on board and for a moment Noah wondered if he was wasting everyone's time. Then a figure appeared high up at the bow and waved at them. Simon raised a hand in acknowledgement – he seemed tense, clearly nervous at getting so near to the superyacht – but the man was waving at Rita, who had begun to wave back. It had to be her friend, the butler.

He shouted something in Russian and Rita called back. Noah sensed she was embarrassed to be raising her voice in front of guests.

'What's he saying?' Simon asked, killing the boat's speed as they came alongside the yacht.

'He wants me to go on board,' Rita said, blushing.

Noah watched as the butler signalled for Simon to bring *Alice Rose* around to the stern, where there was a swimming deck with railings close to the waterline. The next moment, the butler was catching a rope that Simon had thrown him. Once it was fastened securely, Simon helped Rita on board, where she fell into the arms of the butler.

'More than just a friend, methinks,' Simon whispered to Noah, as the two hugged and kissed each other.

'Is it OK if we come on board too, Rita?' Noah asked. He was reluctant to interrupt them, but he knew this might be his only window, his one chance to find out more about Kreshensky.

Rita spoke with the butler for a few seconds. 'Why not?' she said. 'The owner has not arrived yet. They are expecting him this afternoon.'

'Is this such a good idea?' Simon asked.

'We won't be long,' Noah said, trying in vain to sound calm.

17

'WHAT EXACTLY ARE we looking for?' Clemmie asked as she and Noah followed the butler, whom Rita had introduced as Sasha, across the aft deck and into the yacht.

'Anything that links Kreshensky to the hotel, to the mainland,' Noah said.

Noah couldn't believe what he saw: a large backlit bar, made from what looked like white onyx, buttermilk leather sofas and chairs scattered with teal-blue silk cushions, contemporary chandeliers, lacquered walnut and polished marble panelling. A crewmember was busy cleaning wine glasses the size of balloons behind the bar; another was dusting the floor-to-ceiling chrome mirrors on the walls. The decking, Noah noticed, was inlaid with a scattering of precious stones and delicate speckled eggs set in resin.

'Please, it is better you don't touch anything,' Sasha said to Clemmie, who had picked up a crystal fruit bowl and was turning it in her hands.

'Sorry, it's so beautiful,' she said, placing it back down on a low coffee table. She pulled an exaggerated expression of regret at Noah.

'The boss, he likes everything "just so",' Sasha said.

'Shipshape and Bristol fashion,' Noah said. It was good to have Clemmie there. She made him smile, helped him relax.

'Exactly.'

Sasha called out to the crewmember cleaning the mirrors. They spoke in Russian, then Sasha turned to Noah and Clemmie.

'Ivan here will show you around, but we don't have long.' This last comment seemed to be addressed to Rita, who was holding Sasha's hand. They looked at each other, both blushing, said something in Russian and walked off past the bar into another room.

Ivan didn't speak a lot of English, but his brief tour was self-explanatory: they visited the cinema, one of the VIP suites (there were seven in total), the kitchens, a boardroom, a library, a spa and finally the swimming pool and wet bar high up on the spacious foredeck, where he left them sitting on sun loungers, waiting for Sasha and Rita to return.

'We need to take a look around, without company,' Noah said.

'I don't like this place.'

'Me neither. Let's try down there,' he said, getting up from his lounger.

Together, they went over to a door beside a small, outdoor bar and walked down a long corridor lined with doors that were all locked. At the end of the corridor was a door with a glass panel. Noah peered in and tried the handle, which opened. Inside was a fully equipped gym, with a sprung walnut floor and a mirror on the ceiling above the bench press. There were windows on all sides looking out onto Carrick Roads.

The room was empty except for a teenage girl – of a similar age to Clemmie, Noah guessed. She was wearing a Bandier sports bra and print leggings cut off just below the knee, and she was working her biceps with weights.

'Sorry,' Noah said as he stood at the door, trying to look everywhere but at the girl.

'Can I help you?' she said in a thick Russian accent, stopping her exercises to talk. She wasn't smiling.

'We were just looking around,' he said, struck by the girl's high cheekbones and short, dark-cropped hair. 'We're with Sasha.'

Mention of Sasha's name didn't seem to make her any happier. She continued to eye them both suspiciously.

'Let's go,' said Clemmie.

'Your girlfriend?' the girl said, nodding at Clemmie.

The question caught Noah off guard. 'Just friends,' he replied, hoping that he'd said the right thing. Why did he always speak so quickly, without checking himself?

'You like Russian girls?' she asked, smiling for the first time.

Another weird question, Noah thought. 'There are a couple at our school. Very nice. Friendly, hard-working,' he added, talking too quickly, wishing they had just turned around and walked out of the gym. What was he on about? And who was this person?

'Russian girls are stronger than English girls, I think.'

'I wouldn't know.' Noah guessed she was probably right, though, as the girl resumed her weight exercises, flexing taut biceps.

'Shall we find out?' she asked. She wiped her face with a fluffy white towel, tossed it to the ground and walked over to them.

'My name's Valeria, by the way. Valeria Kreshensky. This is my father's boat. We don't get many visitors – strangers walking into our private gym. Welcome.'

Noah shook her outstretched hand, trying not to wince at the strength of her grip. Clemmie did the same, with more reluctance. Valeria's welcome couldn't have been less sincere.

'I'm Noah – and this is Clemmie,' he said.

'Do you arm-wrestle in England?' Valeria asked.

'Not personally,' Noah said, managing a dry laugh. Who was this girl? He was lying, though. He had been challenged to an arm-wrestle early in his first term – by Alexei – and had failed miserably. It had taken a while to earn back the Russian's respect.

'I do,' Clemmie said, moving out from behind Noah.

'Ah, so the English girl speaks,' Valeria said. 'Want to try?'

Valeria walked away to a corner of the gym, where there was a table with four small padded mats, two blue and two red. At either side of the table was a short metal pole.

'Anything to shut her up,' Clemmie whispered to Noah as they followed her over to the table.

'All the crew arm-wrestle,' Valeria said. 'And I've beaten most of them.'

'Girls or boys?' Clemmie asked.

'There aren't any other women on board. So, I put my elbow here...' Valeria demonstrated, resting her elbow on one of the mats. 'And you put your elbow over there. These two mats are for protecting your hand when your opponent slams it into the table. And these poles–'

'Are for holding on to with your other hand,' Clemmie said.

How did she know these things, Noah wondered.

'OK, so you know everything already,' Valeria said.

'I didn't say that.'

Valeria smirked and gestured for Clemmie to stand on the other side of the table. 'Shall we begin?' she asked.

'Clemmie, we should go,' Noah said. Things were getting out of hand. He'd come here to discover what he could about Kreshensky's movements, not get involved in an arm-wrestle with his bat-scary daughter.

'It's fine,' Clemmie said, pulling up the right sleeve of her top.

Noah watched as the two girls linked hands, both adjusting their grip, eyes locked on each other.

'Are you ready?' Valeria asked.

Clemmie nodded. A fraction of a second later, Valeria had snapped Clemmie's arm down hard into the mat.

'Hey, that's not fair,' Noah found himself saying. 'She wasn't ready.'

'It's no problem,' Clemmie said, composing herself. 'Best of three?'

'OK,' Valeria said, surprised. They both settled at the table again, flexing their fingers until they were happy with their grips.

With their free hands, they held on to the poles. 'Ready?' she asked.

'Ready.'

This time Clemmie slammed Valeria's arm over, but not quite as far as the mat, which would have clinched it. Instead, Valeria's hand was suspended two inches above it, shaking. Slowly, very slowly, Valeria began to move her arm back into the upright position and over onto Clemmie's side, an ugly smile spreading across her strained face. At least it would be over quickly, Noah thought.

Clemmie had other ideas, though. Gradually, she swung their linked arms back up to twelve o'clock and, a few seconds later, began to push Valeria's arm towards the mat on her side. They eyed each other, both gripping the upright poles, their entire upper bodies shaking with the effort, until it was all over and Clemmie pushed Valeria's hand into the mat.

Valeria was silent this time, walking around the gym as she flexed her hand open and shut, rubbing her forearm. Clemmie smiled at Noah as she stood at the table, waiting for her Russian opponent to return.

The third contest went on for what Noah thought was an age, but it couldn't have lasted for more than thirty seconds. Valeria had the early advantage, but she had lost the element of surprise and couldn't repeat the snap slam of the first round. Instead, she steadily moved Clemmie's arm over, inch by inch. But then Clemmie seemed to find a new well of strength, brought their hands back to upright and moved Valeria's wrist inexorably closer to her mat.

'My father doesn't like unexpected visitors,' Valeria said, her hand an inch away from defeat.

'Oh, we're going, don't worry,' Clemmie said. 'Once we've finished here.'

The next moment Valeria's arm gave way and Clemmie slammed her hand into the mat.

'We better let you get on with your training,' Clemmie continued, adjusting her top and rolling down her sleeve. 'Looks like you need it.'

'That was a bad idea,' Noah said as they walked out into the corridor and down towards a spiral staircase. 'We need to get out of here.'

'Look at this,' Clemmie said, admiring a huge chandelier that ran down the middle of the entire staircase. 'There must be more than a thousand pieces of glass.'

'Let's take the lift,' he said, turning to the adjacent elevator.

They pressed the basement button and stepped in, sighing with relief as the doors closed.

'When did you learn to do that?' he asked.

'We do it in our house sometimes. On Saturday nights. Sweepstakes, forfeits. Candles instead of mats.'

'Ouch. And do you always win?'

She gave him a withering look. Of course she always won, he thought.

The doors opened and they found themselves in the bowels of the ship. In front of them was an underwater observation room with deep sofas looking out at glass walls. The floor was glass too. Noah found the lights and flicked on a row of underwater spotlights that illuminated the surrounding sea.

'It's like an aquarium,' he said, watching an array of fish swim past one of the ship's stabiliser fins. The elevator doors closed behind them.

'Makes me want to dive in and swim.' Clemmie smiled, rubbing her arm.

'Are you OK? She wasn't very friendly, was she?'

'No surprise with a dad like hers.'

They wandered around the room, marvelling at the sea beneath their feet and all around them. Noah couldn't relax though. They had hardly endeared themselves to Valeria. Clemmie sank back in one of the deep sofas, trying it out for size. Upstairs, Ivan had told them how sixteen different leathers had been used in the bar area seating alone.

'I could get used to this,' she said, admiring the underwater seascape. 'Do you think we'll see any dolphins?'

'Maybe a seal or two.'

Noah wasn't in the mood for small talk. His mind was racing, trying to work out what they should do next. This was their only chance to look around Kreshensky's yacht, establish how he might make contact with the mole.

Clemmie tapped the sofa, indicating that he should join her. She was a little flushed after her arm-wrestling and looking more beautiful than ever. He sat down, perching awkwardly.

'You're OK, aren't you, with us just being good friends?' he asked, still wondering if he had said the right thing earlier.

'Fine by me.'

'I mean, I didn't want to assume–'

'It's OK, Noah, honestly. Relax. We're on holiday. On a superyacht. Under-bloody-water!'

She pulled him back onto the sofa and kissed him. A moment later, the elevator doors opened, making them both sit up.

'You found my favourite room,' Sasha said. Rita was at his side. They were standing against the illuminated glass, silhouetted, as if they were in front of a movie screen. 'You need to go now,' he added. 'We just heard that the owner's flown in already.'

'Flown in?' Noah asked, standing up. Did the boat come with its own helicopter? It wouldn't surprise him if the pool closed over to form a helipad, *Thunderbirds*-style.

'St Mawes. He will be here shortly.'

'Do you know him well?' Noah asked, fishing for information.

'I am his butler,' Sasha said, smiling at Rita. 'A butler knows his boss better than anyone.'

Noah glanced at Clemmie. 'We just met his daughter,' he said.

'So I gather. What did you do to her? She is crazy mad with anger.'

'Just a bit of female bonding,' Clemmie said.

'Has her father got plans?' Noah asked. 'While he's down here?'

'Plans? He only has one thing on his mind while he is here.'

Noah waited for Sasha to explain more, but he said nothing, as if Noah should already know what Kreshensky's plans were. He beckoned them to follow him. They entered the elevator and watched the doors close on the underwater world.

'And what's the only thing on his mind?' Noah asked, trying in vain to sound casual. 'While he's in Cornwall?'

The elevator doors opened and they walked out into the bar area.

'I show you,' Sasha said, 'but we must hurry.'

Another crewman, on the swim deck at the stern of the ship where they had embarked, called out something in Russian. His voice had an unsettling urgency, Noah thought. Sasha barked something back at him and led them through a door beside the onyx bar.

They were now in a corridor, as spotless and shiny as the rest of the ship. Sasha pulled out a bunch of keys from his pocket and unlocked a door. Inside was a small room, its walls full of old, framed pictures – cracked oil paintings of men in naval uniforms. Below the room's only porthole was a glass cabinet full of nautical artefacts: brass and wooden octants and sextants, a telescope. Noah was struck by the strange juxtaposition of ancient and modern – all those naval antiques housed in one of the world's must futuristic boats.

'Kreshensky likes to think of himself as a man of the sea – and a naval historian. He is obsessed with the Spry family,' Sasha said. 'Do you know them?'

Noah shook his head.

'They're a local Cornish family who lived for many centuries near here. One of the ancestors was called Sir Richard Spry.' Sasha pointed at a portrait on the wall. 'Kreshensky is writing a book about him.'

'Why?'

'He thinks he might be related to him. I do not think this is the case – the Spry family are all from Cornwall, not a drop of Russian blood in them.'

'I don't get it,' Noah said.

'Sir Richard was once a very great man in your navy, "Admiral of the White Fleet".'

Noah had assumed – wrongly, he now realised – that the superyacht was called *The White* because of its colour.

'Kreshensky likes to pay his respects once a year, one naval man to another, at a church on the shore where he is buried.'

'Is that why he comes here?'

'He wants to show off his boat, of course, but the reason he visits is to see the tomb of the Admiral of the White.'

Sasha pointed at a photo of a white marble panel. Noah leant in to read the writing:

SACRED TO THE MEMORY OF
SIR RICHARD SPRY, K^T.
REAR-ADMIRAL OF THE WHITE,
SEVERAL YEARS COMMANDER-IN-CHIEF OF H. M. SHIPS
IN NORTH-AMERICA, THE MEDITERRANEAN, AND PLYMOUTH.
HE WAS ENVOY TO THE EMPEROR OF MOROCCO
AND THE STATES OF BARBARY.
HE DIED ON THE 25TH OF NOVEMBER 1775, AGED 60 YEARS.
THIS MONUMENT AS A TESTIMONY OF GRATITUDE IS ERECTED
BY HIS AFFECTIONATE NEPHEW ADMIRAL THOMAS SPRY.

'Sasha,' an agitated voice called out over the ship's intercom system, followed by something in Russian.

Sasha looked anxious. 'We must hurry,' he said. 'Kreshensky will be here any minute.'

Noah and Clemmie followed him down the corridor, through the bar and out onto the swim deck, Rita in tow. The ship's intercom was broadcasting more anxious messages in Russian.

'Where the hell have you been? It's all kicking off here,' Simon said, glancing up at one of the crewmembers. 'I haven't a clue what this guy's saying, but he's behaving like a rabbit of negative euphoria – not a happy bunny.'

'The owner of the boat's on his way,' Noah said. 'We need to leave.'

'I knew this was a bad idea,' Simon said, firing up *Alice Rose*'s engines.

An argument was raging between Sasha and three of the crew. Noah sensed that they were blaming Sasha for having allowed them onto the boat. Sasha turned to Rita, kissed her on the lips and smiled nervously at Noah.

'You must leave now,' he said. 'It may be too late.'

Noah looked out across the water. A rigid inflatable boat, smaller in length than *Alice Rose*, was heading across the water from Falmouth towards them, rounding Pendennis Point with four people on board. He helped Clemmie onto *Alice Rose*, wishing he hadn't brought her with him. There was no need to involve her in this. It was becoming too dangerous.

'Rita!' Simon called, as *Alice Rose* started to move away from the stern of *The White*, slipping around the port side of the superyacht to stay out of sight of the approaching RIB. Rita was having a last kiss with Sasha, accompanied by more shouting from his crewmates. She jumped on board just as Simon accelerated away, heading southwest as a cacophony of Russian expletives faded on the wind behind them.

18

THIRTY SECONDS AFTER *Alice Rose* had pulled away, the RIB came alongside the stern of *The White*. A short man in a white blazer and shades stepped onto the swim deck, remonstrating with crew members, particularly Sasha. Valeria then appeared and kissed him on both cheeks. Noah watched, transfixed, as the man – Kreshensky, presumably – pushed Sasha backwards, stabbing at his chest, until he was about to fall into the sea. He turned to the RIB, looked across at *Alice Rose* and appeared to issue some orders, gesturing with his arms. Seconds later, the RIB sped off, with two men on board, in Noah's direction.

'I think we may have company,' he said.

Simon glanced over his shoulder at the RIB, then reached for a pair of wraparound sunglasses. 'I've always wanted to see what this boat can really do,' he said, putting on the glasses as he pushed forward on the throttles of *Alice Rose*'s Volvo D4 engines, each one delivering 264 horsepower.

Noah watched the GPS display as their speed nudged past twenty knots and the bow began to rise. Behind them, large waves fanned out in a pluming V-shaped wake.

'We can use *Alice Rose*'s weight to carve through the swell,' Simon said. 'RIBs just bounce across the surface. I'm hoping our wake and the chop of the waves will make them come out of the water and go slower. With a bit of luck…'

Noah turned back to look at the RIB as it powered over the crest of a wave. The next moment it had left the water and seemed to hang in the air, outboard engines screaming, before slamming into the next wave.

'It'll flip if they push it too much,' Simon added.

'I'm feeling sick,' Clemmie said.

Noah felt sick too – with fear and guilt, for having involved her. 'Maybe we should just stop?' he suggested. 'Explain what we were doing?'

'No,' Rita said, looking back at the RIB, which was gaining on them. Noah noticed that she was crying. 'You do not know that man.'

Clemmie put a consoling arm around Rita and shot a glance at Noah. Was there accusation in her eyes?

Again, he wondered what he was doing, whether all this was worth it. He smiled at Clemmie, hoping to reassure her, and went into the cabin to join Simon at the wheel.

'Where are we going?' he asked.

'We'd be trapped if we went all the way back up to the Fal,' Simon said, pointing at a chart screen in front of him. 'We could try hiding up one of these creeks…' Noah read the names: Mylor, Pill, Penpol, Restronguet. '… but we haven't got enough of a head start on them. So I reckon we should head over here, to the Helford. It's close to low water and if they don't know this area well, we might be able to lose them.'

Noah glanced back at the RIB again, which was now too close for comfort – barely a hundred yards away.

'They're getting nearer,' he said, noticing how the sea swell had reduced. The RIB seemed more in control, riding the waves better.

'That's Rosemullion Head,' Simon said, pointing at the headland in front of them. 'Around that corner is the Helford – and August Rock. There's a green conical buoy on the seaward side of the submerged rocks. Can you see it?' Noah nodded, but he was struggling to pick it out. 'We're meant to leave the buoy to starboard and then head west up the Helford, but there's a way through, between August Rock and the shoreline, even at low tide, if you know what you're doing. I'm hoping they don't.'

Noah watched as Simon rounded Rosemullion Head and steered for the narrow gap up ahead, following the five-metre contour line on the chart plotter.

'Shout if you see any lobster pots,' Simon added.

'There are loads of them,' Noah protested, despairing at all the small buoys in the water.

'Just the ones in front of us. We've got rope cutters on the propshafts, which should stop us getting tangled. And look out for any slightly rougher water with tidal ripples. That's where the rocks are – hidden beneath the surface.'

Noah did his best as the boat sped through the shallow water. Behind them, the RIB was out in the main channel now, all set to leave August Rock to starboard and overtake them.

'Check the log book, will you?' Simon asked, a new urgency in his voice. 'Over there.'

Noah looked around and spotted a red-covered book on the chart table. He picked it up and read the page at which it was open. Today's date was at the top and, below that, someone – Simon, presumably – had written the time of their departure from Smugglers' Cottage and their arrival at St Mawes Harbour.

'What time did I note down as low water?' Simon asked.

Noah scanned down the page. 'LW: 14.56.' He glanced at his watch. 'Just under two hours' time.'

'OK,' Simon said. Noah was relieved that someone as unflappable as Simon was in charge, but he sensed that even his usual equanimity was under threat. 'Stuff secondary port calculations, this is going to have to be a rough estimate. We need the height of low water over chart datum. What's that figure there, in the white area inside August Rock?'

Simon pointed at the chart before turning back to concentrate on steering. They were travelling at close to twenty-five knots now, the bow throwing up huge sprays of water that sparkled in the sunshine.

Noah glanced over his shoulder at Rita and Clemmie, who both looked pale, and then checked the chart. 'One metre,' he said.

'Two hours equates to three twelfths tidal range – that's about one and a half metres, plus one metre, which gives us two and a half metres of water, give or take,' Simon said, more to himself than anyone else. He seemed to draw strength from the calculations, Noah thought – or maybe it was just his way of distracting himself from the imminent danger. 'Our draught is one and a half metres.' He paused. 'This is going to be close. All we need now is our leading transit marks.'

Noah was struggling. It wasn't the figures so much as the nautical jargon. Simon fell silent before starting to mutter something about mnemonics for compass bearings and variations: 'Cornish Dairy Maids Very Tasty... Or is it True Virgins Make Dull Company?'

What was he on about? Noah cursed himself for not having concentrated more in his navigation lessons at the school sailing club. Ignorance always made him feel vulnerable.

'This is a very narrow gap,' Simon continued. 'We need two marks in line on the horizon. One's the left-hand edge of Gew Rock by that small cove, the second's up on the hill, a distinctive pine tree above Condurrow Farm. When they're lined up, you know you're on the right bearing.'

'OK,' Noah said, without conviction.

'Ask Gee, Mr Ashworth's daughter, when you get back to the hotel,' Simon said. 'She'll tell you all about leading marks – she read about them in *Swallows and Amazons*.'

'Have you been this way before?' Noah asked.

'Toby took me on a port-navigation exercise a couple of months back. Thank God. We made a passage to Fowey and then came across here to the Helford. He showed me the ropes, including how to navigate this gap. Not at twenty-five knots, though, or with a ruddy Russian RIB in pursuit.'

He fell silent now as *Alice Rose* approached the thin strip of water between the mainland and August Rock.

Noah sensed that the moment of truth had arrived. He held his breath, bracing himself against the side of the cabin. Either they would run aground or they would thread through the eye of the needle to the safety of the clear water and the mouth of the Helford beyond.

Simon was gripping the wheel so tightly that Noah could see the whites of his knuckles. 'Tell me what happens,' he said, as *Alice Rose* raced through the narrow gap.

Noah looked behind him, trying to guess what Simon was hoping would happen. The RIB was still in the main channel, but when its crew saw the route *Alice Rose* was taking, it swerved hard to starboard and came inside the rock too. A moment later, the RIB stalled and came to an abrupt standstill, its own wash swamping the vessel. The two men began busying themselves frantically with the outboard engines.

'Speak to me,' Simon said, concentrating on the route ahead as he steered between another cluster of lobster pots.

'They've stopped,' Noah said.

'That's what we like to hear,' Simon said. 'They've probably snagged a lobster pot. Or run aground. There are a couple of smaller rocks in the middle of the gap that I didn't tell you about.'

'And you knew that was going to happen?'

'Hoped, not knew. Only a fool leaves August Rock to port at low water,' Simon said, smiling as he steered south and took them across the mouth of the Helford.

Noah glanced back at the RIB. The crew were still at the stern, inspecting the outboard engines, which were now out of the water. They didn't appear to have looked up or clocked where *Alice Rose* had gone.

'Where are we heading?' Noah asked.

'Gillan Creek,' Simon said. 'We can tuck in out of sight behind Dennis Head. My guess is that they'll either keep going up the Helford, or if they've seen us, they'll think we're heading off round the Nare Point towards Porthallow and the Manacles.'

A few minutes later, they were in the shelter of Gillan Harbour. Noah went back to the stern to talk to Clemmie, who looked pale and shaken. Rita was calm now and had a reassuring arm around Clemmie's shoulder.

'What happened to their boat?' Rita asked.

'She's either run aground or got the rope of a lobster pot wrapped around her props,' Noah said, trying to sound as nautical as possible.

'Sorry about all that,' Simon said, coming back to join them, but Noah sensed that the coxswain hadn't had so much fun for years.

'What are we going to do now?' he asked.

'Sit tight for a bit. They won't find us here. When they've given up searching for us, we'll head back over to St Mawes.'

Noah looked around him and noticed a church on the shore, tucked into the head of the creek. He thought back to what Clemmie had said about her dad reading a book on Cornish churches.

'What church is that?' he asked.

'St Anthony's.'

'In-Roseland?' He was confused, trying hard to get his bearings. His sense of direction wasn't great at the best of times and the high-speed journey in *Alice Rose* had only made things worse.

'St Anthony-in-Meneage,' Simon said.

Noah sat down next to Clemmie. Rita stood up and offered to make everyone a cup of tea. They might not be careering across the water any more, but Noah felt there was still a lot of tension on the boat.

'Are you OK?' he asked, taking Clemmie's hand, which was cold.

'I'm fine when we're stationary or moving slowly.'

'I'm sorry.'

'What are we going to do?' she asked. 'About Dad?'

'Nothing yet.' Noah checked to see if Simon and Rita were out of earshot. They were both chatting in the saloon.

'He'll go to prison, won't he?' Clemmie asked.

'Listen, we've got no proof,' he offered, but he knew his words sounded hollow.

'But we both know it's him, don't we?'

Noah turned away and looked out across the water.

19

SIMON BROUGHT *Alice Rose* alongside the quay at St Mawes, where Noah and Clemmie stepped ashore. There had been no sign of the RIB and Simon had given *The White* a wide berth on their way back from Gillan Creek, but their progress had been tracked by a man with binoculars on the foredeck.

'Terra firma – heaven,' Clemmie said as she set off down the quay.

Noah walked beside her in silence, pleased to be ashore too. One day, when all this was over, he wanted to go back on *Alice Rose* with Clemmie and journey slowly up the River Fal to Malpas, or maybe Truro, travelling at a sedate five knots as they ate a cream tea and played Bananagrams. They would both enjoy that, he thought.

Now, though, he had other things on his mind. Simon's plan was to moor up in St Mawes and wait with Rita for his parents and grandpa to finish their lunch. He'd then take them all back up the Fal to Smugglers' Cottage, where a car would return them to the hotel.

'All we've done is draw attention to ourselves,' Noah said. 'And got Sasha into trouble.'

'What did you expect?' Clemmie said.

'Alexei said that Sasha was our way to get close to Kreshensky, but there was no chance to talk properly. He was more interested in Rita.'

'To be fair, they hadn't seen each other for a year.'

'Maybe there's more to Sir Richard Spry, the naval officer he's obsessed with.'

'That was weird, wasn't it? All those pictures and antiques. Like a shrine.'

'It could be a cover, an excuse for coming ashore.'

'And meeting the mole?'

Two boys went past them on skateboards, heading up towards the car park. Noah thought he recognised them. 'Damn, wish I'd brought my board,' he said. 'There's a skate park up there.'

'We went last year, remember?'

Of course. Noah cursed himself for forgetting. He'd dragged Clemmie over to St Mawes to sit and watch him ride the park's two halfpipes. She had even had a go herself, had let him teach her the basics.

'Fancy some chips?' Clemmie said, nodding across the street at the Watch House, which had a takeaway fish-and-chips counter.

They hadn't eaten their sandwiches, which were still on the boat. Noah's appetite had vanished in all the excitement of being pursued by the RIB, but he was famished now. They joined the queue and watched as the *Duchess of Cornwall* ferry came into the harbour, loaded with passengers from Falmouth. He hoped his grandpa was enjoying his lunch.

As they were walking away, sharing a bag of chips in the sunshine, Noah noticed the RIB coming into the harbour. 'Uh-oh,' he said, nudging Clemmie.

They stood and watched as the RIB, with two people on board, moored alongside the quay next to *Alice Rose*, which was empty. Simon and Rita had presumably gone into town. The two men peered down into the launch, checking if anyone was on board, and then started to walk up the quay.

'I think they might be looking for us,' Clemmie said.

'It's him.'

'Who?'

'Peter Chapman. The one on the left. Recognise him? The guy in the lift, who beat me up on the run – and killed the man in the sauna.'

A moment later, Chapman spotted them and broke into a run.

'Let's move,' Noah said, sliding the chip bag into a bin.

They both sprinted around the corner of the Watch House and up into the car park.

'Is there a way out up here?' Clemmie asked, barely out of breath. She was a good runner, more of a natural than Noah.

'I'm not sure. Maybe a path.' A plan was forming in his head. Not much of one, but at least it was something.

At the top of the hill, he turned and saw his Russian pursuers coming into the bottom of the car park.

'Quick, this way,' he said, crossing over to the skatepark.

There were quite a few skaters around, some kids on scooters too. Noah spotted the two boys who had passed them earlier and went over to talk to them. 'Can we borrow your boards?' he asked. 'Just for a bit?'

They looked at him and Clemmie blankly, but by the time Noah had explained that two men from the local council ('Weirdly, they look a bit Russian – blue eyes, big chins') were trying to close down the skatepark and take him and Clemmie in for questioning, the kids had bought into his plan, keen to help.

Two minutes later, Noah and Clemmie watched from behind one of the halfpipes as the Russians arrived and began talking to the children, asking if they had seen a boy and a girl, indicating their height. Come on, he was taller than that, Noah thought. One of the boys pointed up the hill, as agreed. Noah and Clemmie tensed, ready to make their move. Once the Russians were far enough away, they broke cover and sped down into the car park on the skateboards that the two boys had lent them.

Noah pulled up at the bottom of the car park, waiting for

Clemmie, who was a few yards behind, and saw the Russians at the top of the hill. He looked across the harbour at *Alice Rose*. His parents and grandpa were back on board, along with Rita and Simon.

'Quick,' he said, gesturing at the boat. 'They're waiting for us.'

They pushed off on their boards along the road and swept round to the quay in front of the shops and restaurants. She really wasn't a bad skater, Noah thought, as Clemmie drew up beside him and *Alice Rose*.

'You alright?' Simon asked.

'All good,' Noah said, trying not to sound out of breath. He left the boards behind a lobster pot on the quayside, as agreed with the boys. 'We need to leave.' He pointed across the harbour to where the men were now running towards them.

'I did wonder,' Simon said, gesturing at the RIB moored next to them. 'Maybe release her before you get on board?'

As Clemmie stepped onto *Alice Rose*, Noah undid the RIB's bow rope and let it drop into the water, hoping that his parents hadn't seen him. They seemed engrossed in conversation with Rita, but his grandpa was watching. He'd clocked the two fast-approaching Russians too, and gently pushed the RIB, now free, out towards the middle of the harbour as Noah stepped onto *Alice Rose*.

'All OK?' he whispered, winking.

'All good, Grandpa,' Noah said, relieved as *Alice Rose* accelerated off, leaving the Russians cursing on the quay as their RIB floated away.

20

IT WAS A RELIEF to be back in the comfort and security of the hotel. Noah felt that he was safe here, providing he kept to public places. His parents and grandpa were tucking into afternoon cream teas on the terrace, but Noah had decided to go for a walk in the hotel gardens with Clemmie, down by the tennis court.

Below them the beach stretched out in either direction. Noah could see people on the sand east of the hotel, towards Nare Head, enjoying themselves in the summer sun: games of rounders; two boys throwing a Frisbee; dads digging sandcastles for their children (but really for themselves). He envied the innocence of their holidays.

They found a bench on a patch of lawn, sat down and watched a young couple play tennis. It was bright and breezy today, not too hot. Perfect sailing weather, Noah thought, but he'd had enough of being on the water for one day.

'I asked at reception about Sir Richard Spry,' he said.

'And?'

'He's buried in a graveyard at the church in St Anthony-in-Roseland. It's just behind the Spry family home. I've seen the house before, last year on a walk with Dad. Turrets like a French chateau. Can't miss it.'

Clemmie took out her phone and started to look something up.

'See what you mean,' she said, holding out a photo of the family home. 'I'm sure I saw an identical house in France last year when we were on holiday in Brittany.' She turned to her phone again. 'The church is "the best example in the county of what a parish church was like in the twelfth and thirteenth centuries", according to Pevsner. Still has its medieval cruciform plan, whatever that is.'

'We've no idea when Kreshensky plans to pay his respects to Sir Richard,' Noah said.

'Why don't you get Rita to ask Sasha?'

'Too risky. We have to assume Kreshensky's people are monitoring all phone traffic on the boat – texts, calls, emails, the internet. I should have asked Sasha more about Sir Richard while we were on board.'

'We kind of ran out of time.'

They sat in silence for a few minutes, while Noah tried to think things through. Was Kreshensky planning to meet the mole at Sir Richard's tomb? Use his interest in local history as cover? He was sure that the connection between Sir Richard Spry and Kreshensky was linked in some way to the Russian operation.

'Noah? There's a call for you at reception.'

Noah looked up to see Julie, the hotel's assistant manager, standing at the top of the garden.

'It's urgent – they wouldn't leave a message.'

He glanced at Clemmie, who shrugged her shoulders. 'You'd better go,' she said.

He followed Julie back into the hotel, took the call at the reception desk and recognised the voice at once.

'Hey, my crazy British friend, how are you?'

'Alexei,' Noah said, smiling at the sound of his Russian roommate.

'How is your favourite hotel? Are they still setting fire to the puddings?'

'Crêpe Suzette's on the menu,' Noah said, trying to relax. But he sensed Alexei hadn't called to discuss desserts. 'Where are you?'

'With my guardian in Manchester,' Alexei said. Noah remembered that the last time he was meant to be in Manchester, he'd actually been back in Moscow. He guessed he was calling from Russia now. 'Did you get my letter?'

'I did, yes,' Noah said. 'Thank you.'

'And how's it going?'

Noah glanced around reception. A guest was asking for her room key, another was chatting to Sean at the door. Not really the place to talk about Russian moles within the British establishment.

'It's going OK,' he offered.

'Listen, I think you might have accidentally packed my mobile phone in your bag. The spare one I use at school to order in pizzas and pretty girls – joke.'

'Really? I haven't seen it.'

'If you find it, give it to me next term, yes? And keep eating those pancake Suzies.'

'Crêpes Suzette.'

'Whatever. I have to go now. Take care of yourself. And remember my phone.'

The line went dead. Noah handed the receiver back to Margaret behind the reception desk. What had Alexei been on about? He had unpacked his bag from school and there had been no phone, he was sure of it.

He was about to walk back out to the garden to rejoin Clemmie when Sophie, the waitress who was studying forensics at university, approached him.

'I did some tests,' she said quietly, looking around.

'And?'

She shook her head. 'It's not blood.'

'Oh.' Noah felt a twinge of disappointment. Evidence of blood in the sauna would have made it more likely that James Hilton had been murdered.

'But that doesn't mean he wasn't killed,' Sophie added. She was animated, Noah thought, excited about the case.

'They found statins in his room,' he said. 'He had a heart attack.'

'Maybe he did,' Sophie said, pausing. 'Maybe he didn't. Last term, at uni, we studied an interesting case in Surrey. A healthy forty-four-year-old Russian millionaire died outside his home of a suspected heart attack. He was found face down in his jogging gear. The police decided there was nothing suspicious about his death – even though he was on a Russian Mafia hit-list – but at a pre-inquest hearing a poisons expert from Kew Gardens announced that traces of a rare and very toxic plant had been found in samples of the man's stomach contents, blood and urine. It was all a bit hush-hush, as the discovery made the police look careless, to put it mildly.'

'What was the plant called?' Noah asked as they moved to a quiet corner of the sitting room to continue their conversation. He didn't want to put anyone off their cream tea.

'*Gelsemium*. Otherwise known as "heartbreak grass". It induces cardiac arrest, mimicking the symptoms of an innocent heart attack. The chemical ions in his stomach were like a calling card – they could only have come from a plant of the *Gelsemium* genus. The rarest and most lethal version, *Gelsemium elegans*, only grows on remote mountain slopes in China. It's a favourite choice for Chinese and Russian assassins because it's so hard to detect.'

'But the man from Kew spotted it,' Noah said.

'It was a woman, actually,' Sophie said, smiling. 'I'd better go.'

Noah made his way back out to the terrace, where Clemmie was waiting for him.

'Who was it?' she asked.

She seemed anxious, he thought. Sophie's account of heartbreak grass would only worry her more. He would tell her later.

'Alexei,' he said.

'What did he want?'

'It was very odd. Kept telling me that I had accidentally packed his mobile phone in my luggage and could I keep it for him until next term.'

'Perhaps you did?'

'I'm sure I didn't. Are you OK?'

She nodded over towards the lawn in front of the hotel. A couple had sat down away from the others on the Quarterdeck terrace, at a table made from an old millstone. Noah's heart sank as he recognised the Russian, Peter Chapman, who turned in their direction and stared.

~~~

Clemmie sat on the sofa in Noah's parents' room as he retrieved his suitcase from his cabin. After leaving the terrace, he had headed straight up here, making sure that no one was following him. Clemmie had gone to find her dad before coming on to join Noah.

'Check the side pockets,' she said, glancing through a copy of *Tatler* as Noah put the suitcase on the floor beside her.

He was confident that he'd emptied everything from it the day before yesterday, but Alexei had been insistent. Clemmie glanced at him as his hands felt the shape of something. He unzipped the pocket and retrieved a mobile phone. It was a cheap 'brick' Alcatel, nothing flash, which was unusual for Alexei, who usually bought the most expensive brands. Noah waited for it to power up.

'There's a text message,' he said.

'Read it,' Clemmie urged.

'I can't just read his private–'

'He obviously wanted you to find it.'

She was right, Noah thought. He read the message aloud. 'N, I will call tonight on this phone at 11.30 p.m. Be away from the hotel, somewhere you can talk in private. A.'

He glanced up at Clemmie, who was studying a page in the magazine, a little too intently, he thought.

'It's a clean phone, pay as you go,' he said, turning it off. 'No record of ownership, not being monitored. The message was sent before I arrived, so no one here could have intercepted it.'

'What do you suppose he wants to talk to you about?' Clemmie asked. Noah noticed a new fragility in her voice.

'Kreshensky, I guess. Or maybe Sasha. Is everything alright?'

Clemmie didn't answer. He saw that she was blinking back tears and went to sit next to her, putting an arm around her shoulder.

'Hey, what's up?' he asked.

'It's nothing,' she said, sniffing. A few seconds later, she had regained her composure enough to continue. 'Dad said he has to go out tomorrow afternoon, wouldn't say where.'

'It's probably nothing,' Noah said, trying in vain to play down any significance in her comment.

'There's something else,' she said. 'He was reading a book – *Cornwall's Historic Churches*. He's never been into that kind of thing.'

Noah thought at once of Kreshensky and his annual visits to the local church of St Anthony-in-Roseland, where Sir Richard Spry was buried.

'That doesn't prove anything.' He hoped he sounded convincing, but it was becoming increasingly difficult.

Clemmie got up from the sofa and walked out onto the balcony, her back to Noah. 'I saw the page Dad was reading,' she said.

'And?'

He went outside to join her. They both stared out at the sea in silence. He felt a mixture of dread and, he was ashamed to admit, excitement. Eventually, she spoke.

'It was about the church at St Anthony-in-Roseland.'

21

'I'M JUST GOING to take a walk on the beach, get some fresh air,' Noah said to Andrew, who was on night duty in the hotel reception.

Andrew raised his eyebrows in a knowing way. He probably assumed he was going out for a late-night cigarette, Noah thought, but he wasn't interested in smoking, never had been. 'The stars are amazing tonight,' he added, but Andrew was still suspicious.

Noah glanced at his watch as he walked down the road to the beach. It was 11.20 p.m., ten minutes before Alexei was due to call. His eyes had yet to adjust to the dark and he was grateful for the lights of the hotel behind him, which spilled out into the night, illuminating his way. As he approached the beach, however, the night became even blacker. He turned around and saw that the hotel had been plunged into darkness – there were no lights on anywhere. It was nothing, he told himself, but he was sure some lights usually stayed on; the yellow four-star AA sign on the corner of the building, for example.

He cracked his knuckles and walked on, telling himself to relax, but he was on edge now. The beach was empty except for a couple of glowing white dots down by the water's edge. He assumed they were fishermen and walked over to take a look.

Sure enough, two men were sitting on fold-up chairs, eating sandwiches and drinking from thermos flasks. They each had a long rod, supported on a tripod, that disappeared out towards the sea. At the tip of each rod was a small bead of light.

To begin with they didn't want to talk, but Noah was in need of company and persevered and eventually the men warmed to him and showed him the plastic bag full of sea bass that they had caught.

'This one's forty-two centimetres, the smallest you're allowed to keep,' one of the men said, holding a fish in his hands.

'What are you going to do with them?' Noah asked.

'We'll have one for dinner tomorrow, the others we'll give away to friends.'

Noah watched as one of the rod lights bobbed.

'Just the waves,' the man said, noticing his interest.

Noah nodded and stared out to sea, listening to the lapping water. For the first time he became aware of the clear sky above and the myriad stars scattered across the darkness. There was a fingernail of moon, too, and the lights of ships on the horizon. Then he spotted two pinpricks of light on the rocks beneath Nare Head, close to the water's edge.

'Are they fishermen too?' he asked. There was an entire nocturnal world down here, he thought, while the hotel slept.

One of the men looked up to see where Noah was pointing and went back to eating his sandwiches. 'Husband and wife,' he said, almost in disapproval, as if bass fishing was strictly for men only.

'He's back again,' the other man said, turning on his head torch and shining it down the beach.

Twenty yards away, a fox's eyes were caught in the beam. Noah watched as it stared back at them for a few seconds before trotting off down the beach into the dark. The only other fox he had noticed around here was a statue of one hidden in the rockery, opposite the hotel's main entrance.

'Strange, seeing a fox on a beach,' he said.

Neither man answered. The mood had changed. What else was out there in the darkness, Noah wondered.

He said goodbye to the fishermen and walked along the beach, away from the fox, and checked his phone. Mobile reception was poor in Cornwall, but he had noticed before that the signal was better on the beach. It was 11.30 p.m., time for Alexei to call. He checked that the phone was switched to silent and waited. And waited. Perhaps the text hadn't been meant for him. But it had been addressed to 'N', he reminded himself, and it had mentioned the hotel.

Fifteen minutes later he was about to head back to bed, deflated, when the phone began to vibrate in his hand. He stopped to answer it.

'Alexei?' he said, talking quietly.

'So you found my phone – and read my private text messages.'

Noah wasn't sure if he was joking. Alexei had been known to lose his temper at school – like the time when Noah had borrowed his Yeezy trainers without asking.

'I thought–'

'It's OK, my friend. You were meant to.'

'That's what I guessed.' He wished Clemmie was with him now, but she had been unable to get past the security guards on her corridor.

'Are you away from the hotel?' Alexei asked, more serious now.

'I'm down on the beach.' Noah looked towards the fishermen, who were a couple of hundred yards away. 'There's no one around.'

What if they weren't fishermen? What if they were here to listen in on his conversation? He turned and walked further away from them, to the far eastern end of the beach.

'Tell me,' Alexei said. 'How's it going? Have you discovered the mole?'

'Not yet. But I have met Sasha, Kreshensky's butler.'

'Did he tell you anything?'

Noah paused, disappointed. He'd hoped that Alexei was ringing to give him more information, not to ask questions. 'We didn't talk for long,' he continued, 'but he said Kreshensky is obsessed with a local naval officer called Sir Richard Spry. He was Admiral of *The White* in the eighteenth century, apparently. It's why Kreshensky calls his boat *The White*.'

'And I thought it was because of all that cocaine he snorts.'

Noah glanced around the beach and then above him. A shooting star traced across the scintillant sky, its path so brief that he wondered if he had imagined it. 'Sasha says Kreshensky is going to come ashore and pay his respects at Sir Richard's grave,' he said. 'Maybe that's when he'll meet the British mole.'

'Did Sasha say that? About the mole?'

'No, he just told me Kreshensky would be coming ashore to visit a church.'

The line fell silent for so long that Noah checked to see if he'd been cut off. 'You still there?' he asked.

'I'm here.'

'In Moscow?'

'There was something else I heard my father say that night,' Alexei said, ignoring Noah's question. 'I didn't want to tell you in the letter.'

'What?' The tone of Alexei's voice was scaring him.

'The SVR are involved in this whole operation. Ruthless people.'

'They're here already – staying at the hotel,' Noah said, thinking of Peter Chapman. Alexei had already told him about the SVR, in his original letter. Why was he telling him again?

'Be careful, my friend,' Alexei continued. 'They will kill anyone who tries to prevent Kreshensky from meeting the mole. We have a saying in Russia: no person, no problem. That's how they operate.'

Tell me about it, Noah thought. He'd already been threatened with death on his run up to Nare Head. He knew the Russian intelligence service had form when it came to unusual ways of killing their enemies in the UK. First Alexander Litvinenko, the former FSB agent who had made the mistake of publicly criticising President Putin. And then the Russian millionaire Sophie had told him about. Had James Hilton died of 'heartbreak grass' in the hotel sauna too? It wouldn't surprise him. He would google the case when he had more time, write it up on his website, like he'd done with Litvinenko.

Litvinenko had died a slow, painful death in London in 2006 after a rare and expensive isotope, Polonium 210, was sprayed into the pot of tea he was drinking. His assassins nearly got away with it, but British investigators identified the highly radioactive isotope in Litvinenko's body hours before he finally died. Traces of the substance were subsequently found in a hotel where two former KGB agents had stayed, on the plane they took from Moscow to London, and even at the Emirates Stadium in London, where one of them had gone to watch an Arsenal match.

'I'll be careful,' he said, but he knew it was probably too late. The Russians would have marked him down as a troublemaker as soon as he'd found the listening bug in his room. But would they suspect him of knowing about the mole? He hoped not. He was just a curious fifteen-year-old geek, wasn't he?

'We have another saying in Russia,' Alexei said. 'Sweet lemonade comes from sour lemons. You will make something good come from all this treachery, I am sure of it.'

Alexei hung up, leaving Noah standing in the darkness on the beach. He wasn't sure why his friend had called. Did he regret passing on the information about the mole? Involving him in something so dangerous?

As Noah turned to walk back up towards the hotel, he became aware of someone at the top of the beach, sitting on a bench beside the ramp used to wheel boat trailers onto the sand. He stopped where he was, watching as the figure lit a cigarette with a lighter. The hotel was still in darkness behind him.

It was just someone having a late-night smoke, he told himself. But even from that distance, the man's profile was unmistakable: Peter Chapman. The Russian was observing him with the confidence of an unhurried hunter – calm, confident of making a kill.

Noah tried to think if there was another way back up to the hotel that would avoid having to pass him. If he walked beyond the fishermen to the next beach, Pendower, he could double back along the coastpath that led into the gardens on the west side of the hotel. But it was a long way in the dark and the tide was coming in fast.

He told himself that he was overreacting, but he knew Chapman wouldn't be happy with him. He'd made the Russians look foolish in St Mawes, first when he and Clemmie had outwitted them on skateboards, and then when they had pushed their empty RIB into the harbour.

He walked back towards the fishermen, calculating that nothing could happen to him if he was in company. As he drew near, he heard a noise behind him. He spun around but saw nothing. His heart was beating so fast that he could feel blood circulating through his temples. Then he heard another sound, like a loose rock being displaced. He broke into a sprint down the beach, past the two fishermen, without looking back.

'You alright?' one of them called out.

Noah didn't have enough breath to reply. All he knew was that someone was chasing him. He told himself that only sand lay ahead and he kicked on, stretching his stride. It was difficult running in the dark, though, and he could sense his pursuer getting closer. He veered down towards the sea, barely able to pick out the white of the waves in the darkness. If he was lucky, there would be just enough sand for him to get around the rocks and on to Pendower and then cut up to the footpath at the back of the beach.

But his luck had run out. The tide was higher than he'd

thought. He could either run through the shallow water or scramble over the outcrop of rocks. He headed into the waves, legs tiring, and glanced behind him. It was the other Russian, the one who had stood in the doorway of the farm building while Chapman had kicked him.

For a moment they stared at each other – two humans running like wild animals in the night – before Noah turned away, scared by the deadness in the man's eyes. Why didn't the Russians just shoot him and be done with it? Maybe they wanted to drown him, make it look like an accident. He told himself he was safe, that the fishermen must have clocked that he was being pursued. There were witnesses. But what if they were killed too? Drowned in a freak wave?

He was clear of the rocks now and headed up Pendower Beach, his legs turning to lead as the sand became shingle. The footpath should be somewhere up to the right, leading through a small sand dune. He found it and ran up a flight of wooden steps, three at a time, then turned right onto the road and sprinted again. For the first time he sensed the man behind him was tiring, falling back. The coastpath started again on the bend in the road, through a gap in the hedge on the right where a sign said half a mile to Carne Beach. Three steps and he was onto it, firm grass beneath his feet now, bliss after the soft sand.

He ran along the path, hoping to see the hotel up ahead, but its lights were still off. Once he was on the hotel premises he would feel safer, he told himself, but it was further than he remembered and he felt his limbs growing weaker. When he finally reached the gate, he cut up left through the grounds, ran past the croquet lawn and into the car park.

There was no sound of his pursuer now, but Chapman might have come up from the beach the other way to cut him off. He sprinted through the car park, past the lawn that served as a helipad (for a second he imagined a helicopter waiting for him, blades turning, ready to whisk him away to safety). He kept going down the road, turned into the hotel and ran up to the main entrance. The outer wooden door was locked. He banged on it, peering in through a side window and glancing behind him. Why were there still no lights on in the hotel?

Someone was running down the road. Smacking the doors again, Noah spotted the bell and rang it. Come on, he thought. Andrew must be around, maybe laying up the breakfast tables in the dining room. That's what he did on the night shift, wasn't it? In between checking the hotel for ghosts, as he'd told Noah when he was younger.

A moment later, Andrew appeared and unlocked the door, holding an oil lamp in one hand. Noah fell in, panting hard.

'Lock it, please,' he said.

'Everything OK, sir?' Andrew asked as he relocked the door behind him.

'Not really, no,' Noah said, getting his breath back. 'I was chased by someone on the beach.'

'A ghost, perhaps?' Andrew asked, smiling.

If only, Noah thought, wishing he was an eight-year-old boy again, when summer holidays here had meant sandcastles and ice creams and flying kites with his dad. And what was with all the oil lamps? There were two on the reception desk and others dotted around the hotel lobby.

'It wasn't a ghost. Mind if I hang out here for a few minutes? With you?'

'No problem at all, sir,' Andrew said. 'There's been a power cut, in case you're wondering why we've gone all *Poldark*.'

Noah stood beneath a large portrait of Bettye Gray, drawing comfort from the woman's reassuring presence. Nothing bad could happen on her watch, he felt. A small inscription below read: 'Bettye Gray, 1916 to 2011. A great Cornish hotelier and the inspiration for The Nare.'

'There's a copy of her book over there if you're interested,' Andrew said, nodding at a dresser beneath the stairs.

Noah went over and sat down on a sofa, picking up a hardback of *Oh – Get On!* He needed to take his mind off what had just happened on the beach and tried to read in the light of an oil lamp, flicking through a family tree at the back of the book. His heart was still racing. The late Mrs Gray had bought the hotel in 1989, after running the Edgcumbe in Newquay for many years. Had she ever had to deal with nefarious Russian agents, he wondered? He tried to concentrate on the family tree. Her extended family seemed to run most of the top hotels in Cornwall, as far as he could tell.

'Everyone alright?'

Noah looked up to see Ken, the barman, walking in from the drawing room, dressed immaculately in dinner jacket and black tie, as usual.

'I was just telling Noah about Mrs Gray,' Andrew said.

'A formidable lady,' Ken said. 'The boss's grandmother, as you probably know. Which makes Cordy and Gee the fifth generation. Quite the Cornish dynasty.'

Noah was relieved that Ken had joined them. Safety in numbers, he thought. And there was something particularly comforting about Ken, who was known as Father of the House. He had worked at the hotel for almost forty years and Noah always enjoyed his company. He was urbane, a man of the world, and he told great stories. One of Noah's favourites featured a Saudi prince who'd asked Ken to show him the fleshpots of Plymouth. Ken had apparently donned a full-length fur coat and driven the prince around until dawn. He was just as good with commoners as with kings, though, and he was now looking solicitously at Noah.

'Are you OK?' he asked.

Noah realised that his hands were shaking as he held the book.

'I'm fine,' he said.

'Someone chased him up from the beach,' Andrew said.

Noah told them the bare bones of what had happened,

explaining how he had gone down to the sea to get better phone reception.

'Sounds like you could do with a little something to settle the nerves,' Ken said, disappearing back to the bar. A minute later, he returned with a small glass.

'Cherry brandy,' he said. 'If it's good enough for a teenage Prince Charles…'

Noah took the glass and was about to drink it when he heard a noise outside. Men talking. Andrew glanced at Ken and walked over to unlock the doors again.

'Good evening, gentlemen,' Andrew said as Peter Chapman and the other Russian stepped into the hall.

They said nothing as they waited for Andrew to fetch their room keys. Ken glanced across at Noah and raised his eyebrows. Did he suspect them of being his pursuers, Noah wondered? It wouldn't surprise him. Not much happened in the hotel without Ken's knowledge.

'Is there a problem with the lights?' Chapman asked.

'We've had a power cut, sir,' Ken said. 'Just the hotel. Oddly, nobody else seems to have been affected. Must be something to do with our computer system.'

'How unfortunate,' Chapman said, exchanging glances with the other Russian as they walked over to the stairs.

'Good night,' he said to Noah as they passed – menace in his voice and disdain in his eyes.

Noah flicked through more of Mrs Gray's book, thinking over what Ken had said about the power cut, the look Chapman had given him. As he sipped on his brandy he had an idea.

A minute later, he was in the office behind reception, firing up a laptop he had found, hoping it had enough battery left for what he needed to do. Andrew stood next to him, nervous at having let a guest into a staff area, while Ken looked on. Noah logged into the hotel network on the Cloud. If he was right, the Russians were responsible for knocking out the entire power supply.

Presumably they'd hoped to disorientate him on his way down to the beach, or perhaps it was in preparation for something worse later tonight.

Noah was at ease with computers and soon forgot that Andrew and Ken were with him. He'd started coding a few years back, but it was at his current school that it had become more than just a hobby. His speciality was developing his own smartphone apps, including one that made it easier to bypass the school's pesky internet filters.

His worst fear now was that he would come across a 'hindenbug', malware that could cause catastrophic data destruction, but twenty minutes later he'd undone the damage of what was a fairly crude hack into the hotel's lighting programme. After the main power had been knocked out, a back-up generator had kicked in to keep essential services – fire alarms, telephones, routers – running. It was also meant to power the hotel's external lights and a limited internal lighting circuit, but the Russians had managed to keep the hotel in total darkness.

'That should do it,' he said, sitting back. A moment later, the reception and office lights came up, as if to mark the end of a theatre performance, but Noah sensed there was another act to come.

22

NOAH WAS UP early the next day, the second time this holiday. It was in danger of becoming a habit. His parents weren't used to seeing him before midday, or showing any interest in voluntary exercise. But at breakfast he announced that he wanted to go for a long walk. He explained that he was studying the Second World War at school and that his history teacher, on hearing that he was holidaying on the Roseland, had suggested he visit some old gun batteries at nearby St Anthony Head.

'Are you sure you're feeling OK, darling?' his mum asked, putting a hand up to his forehead.

'I'm fine, Mum,' he said, brushing her hand away. He checked himself. This wasn't the time for moodiness. He knew he was tired. After Ken had walked him up to his room last night he had tried in vain to sleep. Just as he was dozing off in his cabin he'd heard a noise in the corridor. Someone had slipped a piece of paper under the main door. It was a note from Rita, saying that she had heard from Sasha. He was coming ashore with Kreshensky this morning to visit the church at St Anthony.

'I'm just really enjoying history at the moment,' he said, 'and these gun emplacements sound…'

Both parents leant forward.

'Sound…?' encouraged his mum.

'… so fascinating.'

Noah was pleased that they seemed to have bought into his story. They sat back, beaming with satisfaction at his grandpa, as if to say to him: here's a teenager who not only likes to go on walks on holiday but also does his homework – a return, at last, on your costly investment. His grandpa appeared less convinced and gave Noah a wink when no one was looking.

'Clemmie wants to come with me, by the way,' Noah added, as casually as he could, after they had all returned to the table with fruit and cereal from the buffet (and some powdered ginger for his grandpa). He hoped that this wouldn't dent the good impression his parents had formed of him.

His dad glanced across the table at his mum.

'What?' Noah said, indignant.

'Nothing,' his dad replied, but Noah had caught him raising his eyebrows.

Breakfast today was overseen by Alex, a redoubtable Cornish woman who had worked at the hotel for many years (and was the only other member of staff allowed to set fire to the puddings). His grandpa didn't dare flirt with her, Noah had noticed, although she was always full of friendly chat. The oil lamps had gone and full power had been restored, amidst rumours that the hotel's computer system had been hacked, according to Alex, who liked a good story. Noah kept his head down.

His dad tapped him on the forearm to get his attention, nodding as Alex began to hold forth to a group of guests at a corner table. She was talking about Manfred Mann's Earth Band and how she had once gone out with the group's bass guitarist, before he was famous. Noah's dad was always encouraging him to eavesdrop, much to the annoyance of his mum, who thought it rude. 'It's the only way he'll learn about life,' his dad liked to say. 'The things I heard when I was a bairn his age…' He'd even taught Noah how to read upside down – useful if you were sitting opposite someone on a train.

'When I was sixteen, my mum and dad ran the Hillcourt Hotel up the coast at Mevagissey,' Alex was saying. 'Mum used to be the youngest "nippy" at the Lyons Corner House on Tottenham Court Road.'

'What's a nippy?' Noah whispered.

'A waitress,' his grandpa said. 'They worked at the Lyons tea shops and cafés between the wars. Nipped about everywhere in maids' uniforms with matching hats.' Noah noticed a certain wistfulness pass across his grandpa's face.

'One summer, Colin Pattenden – that was the guitarist's name – stayed with his parents at our hotel and we started going out together,' Alex continued, emboldened by her rapt audience, who all seemed to be Manfred Mann fans. 'He played on 'Blinded by the Light', you know. Runs his own PR firm now.'

'Who'd have thought it?' his dad said. 'Everyone has a story.'

Noah desperately wished he could share his, but he knew he couldn't. Not yet. Today was going to be a big day.

After breakfast, he walked down to the hotel library, where he had often gone on rainy afternoons in the past to read or to watch TV on the hidden screen. Today, though, he was on more important business. After Rita had slipped her note under the door during the night, Noah had written a letter of his own, outlining what he was planning to do today, in case he never came back. It was a bit dramatic, but events had become very real in the past few hours and he wasn't sure what Kreshensky planned to do ashore. He'd addressed it 'To whom it may concern', which felt too formal, but if he was honest he didn't expect anyone to find the letter. He hid it inside one of his favourite spy thrillers just in case someone likeminded discovered it in the future and wanted to continue his investigations into Kreshensky and the Spry family.

~~~

Clemmie was waiting for him back at reception and they went out to the car park together to find his dad, who'd offered to drive them over to Place. Noah had told his parents that they would start their walk round the coast from there, towards the Second World War gun emplacements, though they had no intention of actually doing that. His dad was in a strange mood – quiet, though not angry with Noah. As they drove along the narrow lanes, the high hedgerows ablaze with wild flowers, Noah kept an eye on the car wing mirror, in case the Russians were following them from the hotel, but he didn't spot anything suspicious. They hadn't even been present at breakfast.

His dad dropped them off on a no through road that led down to the jetty at Place, just up from the lodge house and the main stone gate to Place House, the Spry family home that looked like a French chateau. He pointed out the wooden signpost beside some stone steps that indicated the footpath down to the church, and beyond to St Anthony Head, and told them to text him when they were ready for a lift back to the hotel. He'd decided to go to Portscatho, he told them, to buy a surprise present for Noah's mum – a picture from the Harbour Gallery.

'Be sensible today, won't you?' he added, glancing from Noah to Clemmie. 'Both of you.'

Oh God, Noah thought, he was about to give them an impromptu chat about sex. 'See you later,' he replied, keen to move away before his dad could say anything embarrassing.

'I mean it,' his dad called out. 'Watch yourselves.'

'Yes, Dad.' Noah sighed. He didn't want to leave on a bad note, but he turned and walked off towards the church without looking him in the eye. He was cross with him, cross with Clemmie, too, he realised. She wasn't holding hands today and they had hardly spoken to each other in the car. She hadn't been at breakfast either, preferring room service with her dad in their suite.

They were now alone as they approached the graveyard in front of the small church. Place House was next to it on the right. The first gravestones were old and covered in moss. At the grave of someone called Henry Higgins, they paused, gazing out over a walled garden. Below that, a large lawn in front of the main house stretched down to a small bay, Cellars Beach, which looked straight across Place Creek to St Mawes.

According to Rita's note, Kreshensky would be coming ashore on the RIB, no doubt mooring alongside the jetty. The tide was almost in. Noah remembered that he had taken a small passenger ferry to St Mawes from here last year with his parents. When they'd returned, the tide had been out and the ferry had dropped them off a hundred yards up the creek at a place called Toddy Steps.

Sasha hadn't been able to give an exact time – all he had said was 'mid morning'. In previous years, apparently, Kreshensky had hired the Place House lawn from Mrs Grant Dalton, who lived in a cottage adjoining the main house, and he had eaten a picnic lunch there, served by Sasha, after visiting the church. There was a marquee on the lawn today – for a wedding, Noah assumed, unless Kreshensky was planning something grander than a picnic – but otherwise the area was deserted.

Clemmie and Noah were still not talking to each other as they walked past the final set of gravestones, which were partially fenced off from the others. Noah stopped to read some of the inscriptions:

IN LOVING MEMORY OF
HARRIET,
WIDOW OF THE LATE
SIR S.T. SPRY, KT.,
DIED NOVEMBER 1ST 1900.

And a much more recent one:

IN
VERY LOVING MEMORY OF
NATHANIEL DUNCAN SPRY GRANT DALTON,
WHO DIED AT PLACE ON AUGUST 25TH 2004,
AGED 82 YEARS.

They were in the right place – the correct St Anthony's church – but there was no sign yet of Sir Richard. Noah assumed the marble memorial plaque, the one he'd seen on board *The White*, must be somewhere inside.

'You didn't have to come today, you know,' he said, suddenly frustrated – annoyed – by her distant manner.

'What, you mean I should just sit around the pool sipping cocktails while you expose Dad as a national traitor?'

'I've told you, we don't know for sure it's him,' he said.

She stopped and looked out across the creek towards St Mawes. A vintage racing yacht – Noah thought he recognised it as a Dragon class – was sailing out to sea, elegant, carefree. A warm breeze was blowing up from the bay and for a moment he wished he was on that yacht with Clemmie, forgetting that any of this had happened. But he knew he couldn't, not now.

'I read something last night, by EM Forster,' Clemmie said, linking her arm in his as they walked on to the church. 'When I couldn't sleep. Dad had been behaving strangely again, trying to give his security the slip. Forster once wrote, "If I had to choose between betraying my country and betraying my friend, I hope I should have the guts to betray my country."'

'What's that supposed to mean?'

'I'm not sure. I guess there are other things in life that are more important, maybe – love, friendship, family.'

'Do you love your dad?'

She paused. 'He's my father.'

'I'm not sure I've always loved mine.' Noah wasn't used to talking about his parents in this way and found himself welling up. 'I do now, though. We're getting to know each other this holiday at last.'

'That's good.'

'It is, yeah. When he's not making embarrassing comments.'

They walked around the southern transept and were about to enter the church door when Noah heard the sound of a boat engine in the distance. He glanced at his watch: 11.15 a.m. They went back through the graveyard to where they could get a good view of the jetty. It was the RIB, the one that had chased them yesterday. Noah pulled his binoculars out of his backpack and focused. He recognised Kreshensky at once, unmistakable in his white blazer. There were two men with him – Sasha, and Peter Chapman – as well as Valeria, the daughter, who was sporting a silver tracksuit. He passed the binoculars to Clemmie.

'What *is* she wearing?' she asked.

'Each to their own.'

Noah looked around them. The best place to hide was on the steep slope above the track to the church, behind some rhododendron bushes. He climbed up first and then helped Clemmie. It was a good vantage point and they watched, passing the binoculars between them like lovers sharing sweets in a cinema, as Chapman tied up the RIB. Kreshensky and his daughter were already on the jetty, walking slowly up the lane that ran alongside the lawn.

Sasha handed Chapman a wooden case – it appeared to be made from a converted wine crate – and stepped onto the jetty carrying a large coolbox, unsteady on his feet. Was it the weight, Noah wondered? He took back the case from Chapman, followed him up the lane and peeled off onto the bottom of the lawn, where he set down the wooden case and coolbox near to the marquee. He then went back to the RIB to fetch some fold-up furniture: three chairs and a table.

Noah's chest tightened at the sound of Russian voices drawing closer. Kreshensky was out of sight now, but he must have reached the spot where his dad had dropped them off earlier. Instinctively, he and Clemmie ducked further down behind the bushes as the Russian came into sight at the far end of the track that led down, below them, to the church.

'Do you think he's going to meet the mole here?' Clemmie whispered. 'It's a bit public, isn't it?'

'Maybe inside the church?'

Noah watched as Kreshensky walked towards them. Which direction would the mole approach from, if he was planning to be here at all? Clemmie was right: Place was too exposed for a clandestine meeting. It was a quiet spot, but at this time of year holidaymakers drove down here to launch their boats or to take the ferry to St Mawes. The church was on the tourist map too. He hated not knowing more. He should have been more upfront with Sasha about his interest in Kreshensky, but there was no reason why the butler would know about the mole, particularly if he was deemed by Kreshensky to be no longer trustworthy.

Clemmie reached for his hand. Kreshensky, Valeria and Chapman were passing beneath them now, barely ten yards away, stopping to look at some of the graves. Neither of them dared to breathe. Noah looked across to the lawn, where Sasha had set up the table and chairs. He was laying out a picnic, removing glasses and plates from the wooden case and food from the coolbox, but he appeared even more unsteady in his actions.

Noah checked on Kreshensky's progress. He and Valeria had moved on up towards the church and were disappearing around the back of the south transept to the front door. Chapman turned, satisfying himself that they were alone, and disappeared too. Noah raised the binoculars to his eyes and looked at Sasha again, this time focusing on his face. He was sweating too much, even for a hot day, and seemed anxious, furtive, a shadow of the happy butler who had welcomed them on board the superyacht. He also appeared to have a black eye and some sort of bruising around his forehead.

'Sasha doesn't look well,' he whispered, passing Clemmie the binoculars.

She watched him for a while and then lowered her binoculars, one hand to her mouth, to see with her own eyes. 'Oh God,' she gasped.

Sasha had collapsed on the grass and was not moving. 'We

should go and help him,' Noah said, checking the church. Kreshensky had only just gone in. If he moved quickly, he calculated, he could break cover and run down to Sasha without being seen. But something made him hesitate.

'I'm going down there if you're not,' Clemmie said.

'Wait!' Noah grabbed her arm. A figure had appeared from the lane and was running across the grass to Sasha.

'It's Rita from the hotel,' Clemmie said. 'What's she doing here?'

'She knew Sasha was coming ashore,' Noah said. 'I guess she wanted to see him.' They watched as she knelt down beside Sasha, cradling his head in her arms.

'I'll go,' Noah said. 'It could be our last chance.'

'What do you mean, "last chance"?'

'He might know something – about the mole.' Noah was shocked by his cold self-interest, but he knew that time was running out.

Clemmie gave him a look. 'I'm coming too – to see if we can help him, help Rita.'

'It's better you stay here,' he said. 'I'll check if he's OK, ask Rita if she needs anything. You need to keep an eye out here, call me if they reappear from the church. We can't afford to be seen by them.'

Her eyes lingered on his for a second. 'OK,' she said. 'Call an ambulance if it's serious. This isn't a game any more.'

'Of course.' He paused. 'It never was – a game.'

He stood up from their hiding place and glanced across to the church before sliding down the steep slope to the path. He turned back towards Clemmie, then set off at a run along the track to the road and Sasha.

Rita looked up as he approached across the lawn.

'Is he OK?' Noah asked, bending down next to them. Sasha's eyes were closed and his head was resting on Rita's lap, but he was still breathing. Rita had tears streaming down her face as she shook her head. 'Have you called an ambulance?' She shook her head again.

Noah dialled 999, giving details of their location and Sasha's condition. He didn't know what was wrong with the Russian, but he described Sasha's profuse sweating, cold skin and weak pulse. When he was told to ask if Sasha could hear him, Sasha managed to open his eyes. A paramedic, the operator said, was on his way.

Noah loosened Sasha's shirt collar and tried to keep him talking, as instructed. He did his best to comfort Rita, too, all the while keeping an eye on the path that led up to the church in case Kreshensky reappeared.

'Sasha, can you hear me?'

Sasha's eyes opened again.

'Rita's here, you're going to be OK. An ambulance is on its way.'

'I'm dying,' Sasha whispered.

'You're doing fine,' Noah said.

He paused before the next question, telling himself that the operator had said he should ask anything that would keep Sasha awake, engage his brain.

'Sasha? Why did Kreshensky, your boss, come here today?'

Rita looked at him, surprised by the question.

'We need to keep him awake,' Noah explained.

'The church,' Sasha whispered.

Noah bent down to put his ear closer to Sasha's mouth. 'What's in the church?'

Sasha struggled to speak. Rita rummaged around in the picnic coolbox and found a bottle of water. She undid the lid and put the bottle to his lips. Sasha drank a few drops, but the rest spilled over his face. Rita mopped it up, sobbing.

'What have they done to him?' she asked. 'Look at him – his eyes, his head, his body. They do this, you know, to those they don't trust any more.'

Noah wondered how much Rita knew about her boyfriend and the man he worked for. Did she know Kreshensky's real role?

Sasha tried to speak again. Noah leant in close. 'Inside the church.' He paused, summoning just enough strength to talk. His voice was almost inaudible now. 'A book.'

'He says there's a book in the church,' Rita interpreted. 'This is why Kreshensky is here.'

A book? Noah looked across the lawn to the house again, and to the church beyond. Kreshensky was still in there, supposedly paying his respects to Sir Richard. What sort of book would there be in a church? A Bible? Hymn book? Prayer book?

'Will you be OK with him on your own now?' he asked.

Rita nodded. 'You don't know these people,' she said. 'It is better they do not see you here.'

'What about you?'

'If they kill me too, at least I will be with Sasha. Thank you for calling an ambulance.'

'No problem,' he said, standing up. 'Are you sure you're OK?'

'Sasha told me about Kreshensky,' she said. 'He doesn't know everything, but he knows enough to help you. Go, do what you have to. For your country.'

23

NOAH SET OFF, running across the lawn to the road, looking back at Rita as he reached the iron fence. He climbed over, ran up the road and turned down the track to the church. As he drew close to where Clemmie was hiding, he heard Russian voices and stopped. It was too late to hide if they came out of the church now. But the voices were further away. He looked towards the bay and saw Kreshensky and Chapman walking down another path that swept around from the house on the far side of the lawn and ran along the bottom, joining the road by the quay. How the hell had they got there?

He turned towards Clemmie, who was well hidden.

'Rita's OK,' he whispered. 'And I've called an ambulance for Sasha. We need to check out the church.'

'Where are they going?'

Noah watched as Kreshensky and Chapman walked across the bottom of the lawn, above a wall at the top of the bay, more than fifty yards from Rita and Sasha.

'Back to the boat.'

'Without Sasha?'

'Looks like it.'

'Murderers!' a voice called out. It was Rita's. 'I hope you rot in hell.'

Kreshensky and Chapman ignored Rita as they walked on to the jetty. Chapman started up the outboard and released the bow rope, and they set off across Place Creek towards St Mawes.

Clemmie came out of her hiding place and ran down the slope onto the track, where Noah caught her from falling down on the other side.

'The ambulance should be here soon,' he said, as Clemmie looked across at Rita and Sasha on the lawn. He knew she thought he had been heartless.

'What did Sasha say?' she asked, following him down towards the small church. A modest lead-and-wood spire rose from the middle of its cruciform layout.

'I asked him why Kreshensky had come here. He mentioned a book – in the church.'

'He wasn't here to meet someone then.'

'It doesn't look like it. But I don't think he came to Place just to pay his respects to the Spry family.'

'Did Sasha know his boss was up to something?'

'He knew enough. He was trying to tell me.'

Noah turned the handle on the heavy wooden door of the church, but it appeared to be closed. Then he noticed the sign saying that it was a stiff latch and he tried harder. This time the door swung open. The interior of the church was beautiful, a refuge of stillness, he thought. Sunlight flooded in from the stained-glass window behind the altar, where there was a simple wooden cross. He walked down to the middle of the church, below the small spire, while Clemmie sat in one of the pews in the nave. They should come to places like this more often, he decided, for the peace and calm.

Now, though, was not the time. He needed to know why Kreshensky had visited here and where he had gone in such a hurry. On the wall to his left, in the northern transept, was an elaborate marble monument: two figures and an assortment of weapons – axes, swords and canon rammers – sticking out from a castellated chest, on the side of which was a family coat of arms. Below it was written:

SACRED TO THE MEMORY OF
THOMAS SPRY ESQ^R.,
ADMIRAL OF THE RED.

Wrong Spry, Noah thought, but he was getting close. To the right was another, more simple, memorial plaque that Noah recognised at once. It was the same as the one he'd seen on board the superyacht, in Kreshensky's room of naval artefacts:

SACRED TO THE MEMORY OF
SIR RICHARD SPRY, K^T.
REAR-ADMIRAL OF THE WHITE.

'It's over here,' he called out to Clemmie. 'Sir Richard Spry's memorial.'

She walked down the nave to join him. They studied it together, Noah running his hand underneath the smooth edges, in case something had been left there.

'If he wasn't meeting the mole here, there must have been a message for Kreshensky, telling him where to rendezvous,' he said.

'What do you think Sasha meant by a book?' Clemmie asked.

'There's no Bible here and there aren't any hymn books.'

'There's a visitors book.'

'Where?'

'By the door.'

Why hadn't he seen it? Why hadn't she mentioned it earlier? He walked back down to the church entrance, leaving Clemmie to study the monument. He flicked through the book. Hundreds of people had left their names and addresses, some adding reasons for the purpose of their visit: 'part of recommended walk'; 'return visit after twenty years'. There was a comments section, too: 'beautiful as ever and wonderful acoustics'; 'a joy';

'so peaceful'. Each entry was dated and there was also a column for the number of visitors in each party: '8'; '2'; '4'; '1'. Noah had no idea the church was so popular.

He flicked through more entries, sure that this was the book that Sasha had meant, but what was its connection to Kreshensky, Sir Richard Spry and the mole? Stick to numbers, he told himself. That was what he was good at. And then it all began to make sense.

'Tell me the date of Sir Richard Spry's death,' he called out.

'25 November 1775.'

Forget the year, Noah thought, as he flicked back through the book: July, June, May. So many visitors. He found November and scanned down the dates, stopping at 25 November. There were six entries, but one visitor's name caught his eye at once, squeezed in beneath the others: 'Harry D Crips'. Three people were in his group, the reason for his visit was given as 'to wish old friends well', the address was 'St Just-in-Roseland', and the comment was 'beautiful graveyard'. It was the name, though, that interested Noah: Harry D Crips was an anagram of Richard Spry.

'He's meeting the mole in St Just-in-Roseland,' he said, heading for the door. 'At 3 p.m. in the beautiful graveyard. We need to be there.'

He lifted the latch, which refused to open first time. He was about to try again when he heard a familiar voice behind him.

'Not so fast.'

Noah spun around. It was Valeria, Kreshensky's daughter. She was standing in front of a small, low door on the western side of the nave, two thirds of the way down, where the pews began. Noah hadn't even noticed the door earlier. He hadn't heard her open it either. Or clocked that Chapman and her father had left the church without her. They must have used this door, which appeared to be linked to Place House, and headed straight through the house and out onto the front lawn.

'Come away from the door,' she said, walking up the stone steps. Noah moved into the middle of the nave.

'I wish I could say it's nice to see you again,' he said, hoping that Valeria hadn't realised that Clemmie was in the church too. Had the Russian been listening to them talk?

'My father wasn't very happy that you came on board his yacht without an invitation,' Valeria said.

Should he just make a break for it, hoping that he could run faster than her? His problem, though, was where to run – and how to get to St Just-in-Roseland.

'Don't even think about it,' Valeria said, reading his thoughts. She pulled out a small pistol from the back of her tracksuit bottoms.

Noah had never had a gun pointed at him before. He thought he was going to faint.

'Pathetic,' she snarled.

Was his fear so obvious, he wondered. He needed to man-up, fast. On the plus side, she didn't appear to know that Clemmie was in the church too. Keep her talking, he told himself, but nothing came out when he tried to say something. Then he had an idea.

'My father, he told me to keep you here for as long as I wanted,' she said.

'The police are coming,' he managed to say, his voice higher than he would have liked. He wished she'd stop waving the gun at him.

'Oh yeah? And why's that?'

'I rang them, when Sasha collapsed.'

'Sasha?' She laughed. 'Why would the police come running? He has a small problem with his heart, I think, nothing more. "Hello, is that the police? My heart is broken. Please come quick." I don't think so.'

Noah really didn't like Valeria. A shocking image of Sasha's sweating and bruised face filled his mind. His plan didn't add up to much, but it might distract Valeria enough for him – OK, Clemmie – to overpower her. By his calculations, the ambulance or paramedic would be turning up any minute now, siren blazing. Valeria wouldn't be able to tell from here if it was the police or a medic.

'Who is your father meeting today?' he asked. He had nothing to lose by asking, he thought.

'I don't know. A private meeting. He was worried that Sasha might have told someone, asked someone along who was not invited. Seems like he was right.'

A second later, the sound of a siren drifted up from the road. She looked at Noah, no longer smiling.

'Wait here,' she said, still facing him as her hand felt around for the front door handle behind her. She tried to turn it, but the latch stuck, just as it had with Noah. She turned around to try the handle again.

Noah knew this was his only chance. He ran at her, grabbing the hand that held the gun, which went off like a firecracker. Had he been hit? He couldn't feel anything. Valeria was strong as they began to wrestle, too strong for him, focused as he was on trying to keep the gun from pointing at his body.

'English men, they are so weak,' she hissed as she began to turn the gun towards him. His wrists were burning with pain. He tried to get his hip behind her legs and twist her body over and onto the floor in a crude judo throw, but it was no good. He told himself he must go to the gym next term. Do some bench presses like the proper rugby players, pump some iron. If only he knew where the gym was.

A moment later, the gun was flying through the air. Clemmie had run over and kicked it out of Valeria's hand. He looked up as she grabbed the Russian's hair, pulled her head back and cracked it down onto her raised knee. Valeria slumped to the ground, holding her nose. Noah tried to look away, but he was transfixed by Clemmie, who kicked Valeria in the stomach as she fell forward.

'Ouch,' he said, wincing. 'I had her, you know.'

''Course you did,' Clemmie said.

He was trying to make light of what had just happened, as he always did in extreme situations. In truth he was petrified, breathing hard, his whole body shaking, particularly his arms. He had very nearly been shot.

He looked down at Valeria's body on the tiled floor. 'Will she be OK?' he asked, his voice quieter now.

'She'll live. Which I suspect is more than can be said for Sasha. Grab her legs.'

Noah hesitated, watching as Clemmie slid her hands under Valeria's armpits.

'What are you waiting for?' she asked.

He lifted her legs up and together they carried Valeria's limp body down to the front pew, where Clemmie sat her up. Her eyes were still closed, but she was beginning to regain consciousness. Noah didn't want to linger on her face, which was a jellied mess.

'Get one of those kneeling cushions from over there,' Clemmie barked as she kicked off her shoes.

'What are you doing?'

Clemmie had peeled off her tights and was tying Valeria's arms behind her back with them. 'Kneeler. Quick,' she said.

Noah retrieved a cushion from another pew and put it on the floor in front of Valeria, frightened now by Clemmie. Without hesitating, she moved Valeria's body forward into a kneeling position and hog-tied her hands to her ankles with what was left of the tights, forcing her body to arc backwards in some sort of weird yoga pose. She then propped her against the pew. It didn't look comfortable.

'I suggest you pray for forgiveness,' she whispered into Valeria's ear. 'For whatever you and your father have done to Sasha. Rita loves him very much, you know.'

Valeria rolled her vacant eyes at Clemmie and spat out some blood.

24

NOAH WAS PLEASED to be out in the daylight again. They ran down the track from the church and joined the road that led to the slipway. An ambulance and a paramedic motorbike were parked halfway down and they stopped to talk to a tearful Rita.

'They don't know what's wrong with him,' she said.

'Is he conscious?' Noah asked.

'He's talking. Not making much sense. People like Kreshensky, they can kill people from the inside and nobody ever finds out how.'

Noah remembered what Sophie had told him, about the Russian who had been murdered with heartbreak grass. He jumped over the iron fence and went across to where two paramedics were kneeling beside Sasha. One of them looked up as he came over.

'How is he?' Noah asked.

'Friend of yours?'

Noah nodded.

'We're taking him over to Truro once he's been stabilised.'

Noah bent down and looked at Sasha, who seemed worse than before and was sounding delirious, mumbling something in Russian.

'Thanks,' he said, hoping Sasha could understand him. He doubted it though. 'We found the book.'

Sasha turned his head towards him and smiled.

'Get the hospital to check his body for traces of a plant called *Gelsemium elegans*,' Noah said to the paramedic, who repeated the words back to him before writing them down on a notepad.

He walked over to the road, upset by how ill Sasha was, hoping that he might be saved if the doctors knew what was wrong with him. Clemmie had gone on ahead to the jetty, where she was waiting for him.

'We've just missed it,' she called out as Noah jogged towards her.

The St Mawes passenger ferry, a small launch, was heading out across Place Creek with six people on board. He turned to look at the timetable beside the slipway. The next ferry wasn't due to leave for another half an hour.

'We need to find a way across,' he said, glancing around at the other boats on the slipway and those moored in the creek.

'We could swim?' Clemmie offered. 'It can't be more than a few hundred yards.' She could – she swam for the school, of course – but Noah had just spotted a tender on the slipway. 'TT *Maggie O'Nare*' was written on the stern, which rang a bell. A couple of years ago, he and his dad had been taken out for a sail in a Cornish Crabber by Toby Ashworth. The boat belonged to the hotel and he was sure it had been called *Maggie O'Nare.*

A minute later, they were lowering the tender into the water. The oars and rowlocks had been stored underneath the boat. He might not be the strongest arm-wrestler, but Noah was good with an oar.

'When did you learn to row?' Clemmie asked, watching him from the small seat in the stern as they set off across the creek towards St Mawes.

'Dad taught me,' he said, pleased that he seemed to have found something that he was better at than her.

'Not bad,' she said.

They were cutting through the water as fast as Noah could go – until one of the oars popped its rowlock and he slipped backwards off his seat. She didn't seem to mind, but he was annoyed with himself for showing off.

He was soon back into the rhythm of rowing and the calmness of the beautiful creek allowed him to order his thoughts and work out what he was going to do next, although he was still haunted by the look on Sasha's face. He would be dead by the time they reached the hospital, Noah guessed.

'What are you thinking about?' Clemmie asked.

'Sasha,' he said. 'And Rita.'

'Me too.'

'She'll never get over it.'

Sasha's imminent death made Noah more determined than ever to expose Kreshensky for what he was: a cold-blooded killer who was undermining a country that Noah now realised he loved more than ever. On a cloudless day like today, in a place as beautiful as this, with Clemmie at his side, he couldn't think of anywhere in the world he'd rather be.

His plan, once they were across at St Mawes, was to leave the tender on Summers Beach, jog round to the castle and follow the coastpath up to St Just-in-Roseland. He had walked the route before with his parents. It was no more than a couple of miles and should only take them twenty minutes if they got a hoof on. They had enough time too. It was just gone 1 p.m. and, if his decoding of the visitors book was correct (number of visitors in party = time of meeting), they had until 3 p.m. to reach the graveyard at St Just.

'Thanks,' he said, fixing his eyes on Clemmie as he rowed. 'For back there. You know, with Valeria. I didn't have her.'

'I'm sure you did,' she said, smiling.

'When did you learn to do all that stuff anyway?'

'I was a bit of a tomboy when I was younger. Always getting into fights – with boys.'

'Right,' Noah said, making a note never to pick a fight with her. An image of Valeria's bloodied nose came and went.

~~~

Fifteen minutes later they were jogging along the coastpath towards St Just-in-Roseland. There were a few walkers, but most people seemed to have headed for the beach or the water – Carrick Roads beside them was a patchwork of pastel dinghy sails.

'Dad said he was going off for a walk this afternoon,' Clemmie said, as they stopped for a breather. She seemed more nervous than out of breath, Noah thought.

'Did he say where he was going?' he asked.

There was a pause before Clemmie answered. 'To look at some churches on the Roseland.'

'With his security, I assume?'

'If he hasn't given them the slip again.'

'There's no way a serving Home Secretary would meet up with an agent of the Russian state in broad daylight,' Noah said, pleased by how authoritative he sounded. She seemed to be reassured.

They set off again, running alongside each other in silence, occasionally falling into single file when the path narrowed. When they reached Pasco's Boatyard, the public right of way ran across the hardstanding in front of the small yard. A hairy lurcher came out of a shed to greet them with a half-hearted bark. Noah looked in on the yard as they passed. A bearded man in blue overalls was on a stepladder, varnishing the gunwales of an old wooden fishing boat.

'Watch the roots,' Noah called over his shoulder as they rejoined the path on the other side of the yard, the lurcher in tow. The path rose up away from the shoreline into the trees and they could see a sandbar ahead that curved out into St Just Creek. Noah remembered the scene, not from walking here with his parents but from one of his mum's paintings that hung on the landing at home.

They stopped at a gate where a sign read: 'Dogs on leads, please – consecrated ground.'

Noah turned to the lurcher, ruffling its ears. 'You're very lovely, but you need to go back now,' he said. The dog looked at him, cocking his head to one side, and slunk back down the path towards the yard.

'Rejected,' Clemmie said. 'How could you?'

'We haven't got long,' Noah said, opening the gate. Now wasn't the time for sentimentality.

She followed him through and they entered the churchyard. He remembered the place better now. Gravestones were dotted across the hillside beside them. A network of paths meandered up through the trees, giving mourners access to the graves of their loved ones.

'Magical, isn't it?' he said. He had stopped beside two towering pine trees.

'What a beautiful place to be buried,' Clemmie agreed.

To their left, a small channel ran around the far end of the sandbar and opened out into a still pool of water where several yachts had moored, their owners enjoying the sunshine. A white wooden boathouse was perched on the far bank, timeless in its simplicity. Noah recognised the building from another of his mum's paintings. Ahead of them, where the footpath dropped down to the shore again, they could see the church, surrounded by palm trees and other lush, tropical-looking vegetation whose names Noah didn't know. A black-and-white Cornish flag billowed from the stout stone tower.

'It used to be a botanical garden,' he said, glancing at a shared gravestone on the bank beside them. 'I came here with my parents once.' The gravestone commemorated Winn and Henry Maddick; the latter had lived for ninety-nine years. Noah didn't know how long he wanted to live, but he knew he hadn't wanted to die when Valeria pointed the gun at him in the church.

'Did the visitors book say where Kreshensky might be meeting the mole?' Clemmie asked.

She was being brave about this, Noah thought.

'The only clues were "St Just-in-Roseland" and "beautiful graveyard",' he said, removing his binoculars from the small backpack he'd brought with him. 'And the time – 3 p.m.' He was sure he was right about the message in the visitors book: Kreshensky was using one church to arrange a meeting in another. Perhaps there was a visitors book here, too, with a message to meet in a third church. It would fit with Jack MacKenzie's apparent interest in Cornwall's churches. Noah's theory, though, was that Kreshensky would meet with the mole here. He just wasn't sure where.

He lifted the binoculars to his eyes again and scanned the shoreline, then swept the path in front of the church, the pool, and the hillside behind the church. Perhaps they would meet on one of the many paths that wound through the trees and gravestones. Had he missed something? A clue to a particular gravestone? He thought back to the time he'd come here with his parents and remembered that they'd gone to look at a well.

'Of course,' he said. '"To wish old friends well."'

'What?'

'That's what it said in the visitors book. "Reason for visit: to wish old friends well." They're meeting at the well, over there, on the far side of the pool.'

Noah kept his eyes on the bank, to the left of the church, and passed the binoculars to Clemmie.

'There's a path that leads up from the shore to the well. See it?'

'I can see the path.'

'The well's at the far end, in a small hollow. Halfway down the path, on the right, there's a set of wooden steps cut into the bank that goes up to a car park on the far side of the gardens.'

'I can see someone by the well,' she said. 'I think it's Kreshensky.'

Noah took the binoculars from her and focused. It was the oligarch, in a shirt and chinos, no longer wearing his white jacket. He was on his own, waiting, smoking.

'What's the time?' he asked, watching Kreshensky as he paced up and down the path.

'Three o'clock.'

'There's someone coming.' Noah's hands tightened on the binoculars. 'Down the wooden steps.'

'Please God, tell me it's not Dad,' Clemmie whispered, her voice weak with emotion.

'It's not,' Noah said, swallowing hard as he tracked the figure walking down the steps towards Kreshensky. He could only see the shoes – familiar shoes. Now the legs. Legs he recognised. Now the whole person. His heart flipped.

25

'IT'S MY DAD,' Noah said, transfixed by the sight of his own father shaking hands with Kreshensky.

Dad? It couldn't be, but it was.

Both men looked around as his dad held Kreshensky's hand – for longer than was necessary, Noah thought. Had something small, a USB stick perhaps, just been passed between them?

Noah's hands were shaking too much to see any more. Clemmie took the binoculars as he slumped over, hands on his knees, and retched.

Dad?

'Oh my God,' Clemmie said, looking at the scene across the bay. 'I'm so sorry.' She lifted Noah upright and held him close.

Noah was fighting back the tears, trying to work out what this meant. He couldn't begin to comprehend the implications. His dad? A traitor? Passing secrets to the Russians? What would he tell Alexei? How would he confront his dad? And would Clemmie tell her father?

He unpeeled from her embrace – already he could feel a distance growing between them – and took the binoculars again, in case he'd been imagining it all. But no, his dad was still talking to Kreshensky. They had walked up the path to the well now, out of sight of the church and the bay and barely visible from Noah's vantage point. It was a secluded spot, ideal for a clandestine meeting. Noah tracked the binoculars across to the church and then back to the well and beyond. There was no one else around. He panned across the bay and saw the Russian RIB coming through the gap between the far shore and the sandbar. Chapman was at the wheel, no doubt back to pick up Kreshensky.

'Chapman's here,' he said, gesturing at the RIB, which had pulled up in the middle of the pool, thirty yards offshore. They were well hidden from him, behind their pine trees. Did Chapman know who Kreshensky was meeting? He looked back at his dad again, the man he had thought he was getting to know this summer, the father who had brought him up. He felt more of a stranger to him than ever. Shock was already giving way to anger. How could he do this to him? To his mum? To his own country?

It looked like their short meeting was coming to an end. Noah watched as they shook hands again, hugged – Oh, Dad – and went their separate ways, his dad disappearing up the steps, Kreshensky walking back to the shore, where he gestured for Chapman to pick him up. Noah couldn't watch any more and walked away, up through the gravestones and trees, trying to make sense of it all. His dad was dead to him now, that's all he knew.

~~~

Noah and Clemmie hardly spoke as they walked along the road, hoping to hitch a ride back to the hotel. He couldn't blame Clemmie for the sense of relief she clearly felt. For ages she'd thought her own father might be a traitor. Now, though, her dad was in the clear and their relationship was safe, unsoured – unlike his with his dad.

Noah had decided he would confront him as soon as they got back to the hotel.

'Just give me half an hour before you talk to your dad,' he said.

'Who says I'm going to talk to anyone?' she replied.

'If he's a traitor, let me announce it to the world first.'

'You don't have to, you know. Tell anyone.'

'What? And just pretend it never happened?'

'What would you have done if it had been my dad who met Kreshensky?'

Noah paused. He'd wrestled with this ever since Jack MacKenzie had come into the frame.

'I would have let you decide.'

'And I'll let you choose,' she said. 'This is our secret. No one else needs to know.'

'Really?'

'Sure.'

She took his hand as they walked along the road in silence. Noah was beginning to suspect that he could never go public about his dad. It would be another betrayal, and there had been enough of those already. Right now he just needed to be sure that Clemmie wouldn't talk to her father before he had had a chance to speak with his dad.

'I can't expect you to be a part of this,' he said, testing her offer of secrecy, giving her another chance to go her own way. 'You'd be aiding and abetting a criminal if you didn't tell someone – your dad's the bloody Home Secretary.'

'And your dad's your own flesh and blood, Noah. Nothing's more important than that.'

He squeezed her hand, grateful for the support. It bought him time. He might not be close to his dad, but he knew him well enough to be sure that there must be more to his meeting with Kreshensky. Another side to the story. There always was. He was angry, a part of him wanting to punish his dad for all the missed school plays, the holidays he was never there for, but already his confused rage was giving way to a burning desire to find out why.

26

THEY HAD BEEN walking along the lane for twenty minutes when a car slowed behind them. Clemmie turned first. Noah was still lost in his thoughts, but he recognised his dad's car at once as it overtook them and came to a halt twenty yards down the road. He glanced at Clemmie, who gave him an encouraging look, and went up to the driver's door. The electric window lowered.

'Get in,' his dad said. 'Both of you.'

His tone was authoritative, not like his usual distant self. Noah had prepared what he was going to say, but he hadn't expected his dad to be on the front foot like this. He fell silent as he opened the rear door, gesturing for Clemmie to go round to the other side.

He didn't want to look at his dad in the rear-view mirror, but his dad kept glancing at him as the car pulled away. Something wasn't right. Did he know that they'd seen him meeting Kreshensky? Was that it?

He needed to take the initiative, get back on equal terms. 'We were at St Just in-Roseland, just now,' he began.

'I know,' his dad said.

Noah glanced across at Clemmie. 'We saw you meet–'

'You don't have to explain,' his dad continued.

'I think it's you who needs to explain, Dad,' Noah said, his anger rising. 'What the hell were you doing meeting Kreshensky?'

'I'll explain. Everything. I promise. First you need to tell me why you were there – how you knew.'

'I didn't know... that it was you.' Noah had expected to be in full flow by now, raging at his dad, telling him how little he loved him, but the atmosphere in the car was weird; it was almost as if his dad was debriefing him after a school exam.

'But you knew Kreshensky was due to meet someone at St Just-in-Roseland,' his dad said. 'How?'

'How did I know Kreshensky was going to be at St Just?' Noah was dismayed by the raw emotion in his voice, happy to repeat his dad's words rather than try to order his own. The events of the past few hours were catching up with him: Valeria nearly shooting him, Sasha at death's door, his dad unmasked as the traitor.

'Tell me,' his dad said. 'It's important.'

'Because Rita, at the hotel, her boyfriend works for Kreshensky and...' He faltered, unsure whether to tell his dad about Sasha. Tears were welling. It felt disloyal – to Sasha and to Rita. More betrayal. If his dad was working for the Russians, he had no desire to put Rita in further danger. She had already suffered enough.

'How did you know where the meeting place was?' his dad pressed.

Noah glanced again at Clemmie, who nodded at him, as if to say it was OK to keep talking.

'Kreshensky is interested in the Spry family – as I found out when I went aboard his superyacht while you were having lunch in St Mawes. I discovered that he would be coming ashore to pay his respects at the Spry family church in St Anthony-in-Roseland. We saw him go there and found a message he left afterwards in the visitors book, suggesting that he would be "wishing old friends well" at St Just-in-Roseland.'

'And then you waited,' his dad said, seemingly impressed. 'For whom?'

Noah paused. 'For the traitor. Alexei, my roommate, he was the one who started all this. Told me that there's a mole high up in the British establishment, that Kreshensky is his handler.'

The faintest of smiles played across his dad's lips as he drove on in silence, along the narrow, high-hedged lanes familiar to them both from past years, when Noah's summers had been such uncomplicated affairs and family choices so simple: which beach today, where to walk, was it to be lunch or morning coffee at the Hidden Hut café?

'I need to know why, Dad. Kreshensky's poisoned Sasha, Rita's boyfriend. He might be dead by now, for all you care. And his daughter, Valeria, she nearly shot me.'

'But she didn't,' his dad said, glancing in the mirror at Clemmie. 'I think she was...' He paused. 'A little tied up.'

His dad clearly knew far more than he was letting on. Noah took Clemmie's hand. They were driving down the lane to the hotel now.

'I will explain everything,' his dad said. 'First I need to talk to your father, Clemmie.'

'What, and steal some state secrets?' Noah said.

His dad ignored him. 'It's essential you tell no one what's happened, what you saw. Is that clear?'

'Why shouldn't I?' Noah said. He felt stronger when he was angry, less vulnerable.

His dad pulled into the top car park, below the patch of grass that doubled as the helipad. He switched off the engine and turned round to face Noah.

'Because I'm not working for the Russians.'

'What?'

'Meet me up beyond Nare Head in an hour. Alone. You know the place.'

27

NOAH COULD PICTURE the scene as they followed the footpath through the bushes and inhaled the faint scent of coconut from the yellow gorse flowers. His dad would be sitting on the simple wooden bench that looked out to sea. It was a favourite place for both of them; they had sat there together many times before, usually in awkward silence after his dad had tried to talk to him about the dangers of sex, or drugs, or online pornography.

After they'd got back to the hotel, Noah and Clemmie had lain for a while on his parents' bed, staring up at the ceiling, stunned by his dad's involvement with Kreshensky and his subsequent claim that he wasn't working for the Russians. What did that mean?

He could sense Clemmie's palpable relief that it wasn't her dad. That there was nothing significant in the Home Secretary's choice of holiday reading – *Superyacht Monthly* and *Cornwall's Historic Churches* or his solitary walks after he'd given his bodyguards the slip. Clemmie surmised that he'd just wanted some time alone, to grieve and to remember her mum. And Noah was grateful for the kind words that she'd offered him. There had to be a good reason for his dad's actions and, either way, she was adamant that she wasn't going to tell anyone.

They had been silent for much of the walk up to Nare Head, until they reached the top, where Noah started to talk about the area's past, recalling stories that his grandpa had told him. He felt he was on safer ground: black-and-white historical facts that he could understand, not the confusing, penumbral world of espionage that they both now found themselves in.

'Up ahead is the site of an atomic early-warning bunker, built at the height of the Cold War,' he said as they stood for a minute after the steep climb, a group of sheep eyeing them from the path. He wasn't sure why he was telling Clemmie this, or if she was even listening. 'When I was younger, I used to come up here with a home-made pinhole camera, ready to capture the flash of a nuclear strike.' Noah paused, glancing at Clemmie. 'As you do. That was their role, you know, the people who lived down in these bunkers. Can you believe it? Monitoring complex nuclear fission with basic pinhole cameras.'

'Your dad's waiting,' Clemmie said, 'over there, the grassy mound.' She nodded at a figure in the distance, standing beside a bench in running gear.

His dad turned and lifted a hand in greeting. Clemmie waved back. He cut a lonely figure, Noah thought. Perhaps he was going to tell him something else. Were he and his mum separating? He prayed not. So many of his friends at school had had to deal with divorcing parents, divided Christmases, two bedrooms.

'That mound's actually another bunker,' Noah said, as they walked on through the gorse, scattering sheep ahead of them. Noah was burbling, quicker now, in the style his mum called 'argle-bargle'.

'Built in the Second World War and manned by Royal Navy crewmen. They operated a network of decoy lights and film studio special effects all around here. Meant to mimic the lights of Falmouth docks.'

He stopped, pointing across the bay towards Falmouth in the distance. Clemmie remained silent. She must be bored and he should stop now, he thought, talk about the weather, school, but he couldn't help himself. 'As German bombers approached by night, their pilots were fooled into thinking Nare Head was Falmouth, so they dropped their bombs all around here, in the wrong place. Genius, eh? Fake explosions convinced the Germans they'd hit their targets.'

Noah stopped. They were still a hundred yards from his dad. It was windy and Clemmie had to keep sweeping strands of hair out of her eyes.

'Sorry,' he said, taking her hand. 'For the war stories. For rambling on. I get it from my grandpa. I'm nervous.'

'I know you are.' She leant forward and kissed him on the lips. 'Me too. I'll leave you to it. Your dad wanted to meet you by yourself. Come and find me afterwards, on the headland,' she said, pointing back at Nare Head, where it overlooked the bay. Noah watched as she walked away.

~~~

His dad shuffled up on the bench to make way for him, as if they were waiting for a rural bus to arrive. His manner was more relaxed than Noah had been expecting.

'You ran,' Noah said. He clicked the knuckles of his right hand, one by one, and then started on his left hand.

'Always do, after meeting Kreshensky. That or a shower. Something to cleanse body and soul – and lose my tail. Were you followed?'

'I don't think so,' Noah said, glancing around him. He had checked once or twice on the walk up from the hotel, tensing as they'd passed the hut where he'd been beaten up. His dad must have come another way, looping around inland.

'What I'm about to tell you cannot be repeated to anyone,' he began, his tone more formal. 'I should ask you to sign the Official Secrets Act first – you will have to sign it shortly – but, well…' He paused, managing a small laugh. 'You're my own son.'

Noah felt a lump rise in his throat. He looked out to sea, where seagulls circled a large outcrop of rock. 'I need to know what's happening, Dad.'

'I know you do.'

The silence that followed reminded Noah of earlier chats here, but his dad was never one to be rushed. Noah twisted his long legs into an awkward tangle.

'If you're not working for the Russians,' he said, his voice tentative, searching for a way through his confusion, 'why did you meet up with Kreshensky?'

'Because he thinks I am working for them.'

'But you work for the Office for National Statistics.'

'I'm employed by the Security Service, Noah. MI5. Have been ever since I left university.'

Noah wondered if he was going to cry as his dad's words hung in the wind like the seagulls out at sea. A number of explanations, including this one, had crossed his mind as he and Clemmie had walked up to Nare Head, but he hadn't allowed himself to entertain it for more than a few seconds. The implications were too overwhelming. A lifetime of lying, commuting to a fictitious job. But he wasn't cross with his dad. He wanted to hug him. Instead, they continued to sit on the bench next to each other, their bus yet to arrive.

'So Clemmie's dad is your boss,' he managed to say, his voice so quiet he didn't expect his dad to hear him.

'I report directly to the MI5 DG – and, yes, he answers to Jack MacKenzie.'

Noah paused. 'All these years,' he said. 'Why didn't you tell me?'

'God, how I wanted to, believe me. Watching your passion for espionage blossom, I was like any proud father. It killed me inside, pretending I didn't care, but it was important you knew nothing. Not until you were ready.'

It was almost too much for Noah to take in. So much for the

seemingly distant dad. In fact they were more alike than he could have dared to believe, just unable to share the one thing they had in common, their relationship blocked by what should have bonded them. He would have preferred a dad who worked for GCHQ, but he could live with MI5. Perhaps he could be seconded to Cheltenham. Maybe he already had been. So much to ask. First, though, Noah needed to understand why his dad had been at St Just-in-Roseland meeting Kreshensky.

'If Kreshensky thinks you are working for the Russians, but you're not and you work for MI5, that makes you a...' Noah faltered, unable to say the two words that he had only ever read in the pages of a spy thriller.

'The Russians know that I work for MI5, that I have quite an important role, which is why they approached me.'

Noah remembered Alexei's original words. *Someone very senior in the British establishment.*

'Their approach was not a surprise. We had suspected for some time that Moscow was fishing for senior UK intelligence and military figures to turn. So we set about playing up my credentials. I had dabbled briefly in some far-left, quasi-communist politics at Sussex University, which had caused me a few vetting problems when I was joining MI5.' He coughed up a short, dry laugh at the memory. 'Let's just say I got back in touch with some old comrades.'

'And the Russians took the bait,' Noah said.

'I only pass on information we want them to know. Sometimes it's nothing – "chicken feed", as we call it – and sometimes it's more important.'

'Disinformation?'

'Not always. A few years back, we intentionally leaked a lot of genuine and highly confidential information about nuclear contamination and how to control it. We knew they were struggling to clean up Chernobyl. Channels like mine were used to help them, without anyone losing face.'

His dad paused before continuing, retying a lace on one of his running shoes. Noah sensed another surprise coming.

'It was Alexei's father who recruited me.'

'What?' Noah cracked a knuckle, his brain racing ahead, trying to compute the implications.

'When he was posted to the Russian embassy in London. He was head of the SVR residency here.'

'But he's one of the good guys, isn't he? A renegade. Alexei's always telling me how much his dad hates working for Putin.'

'Alexei's been lying. An understandable response for a Russian teenager studying at boarding school in Britain, where Putin is not popular.'

'Does he know what his father does?'

'Alexei works for him.'

Noah paused. 'I don't understand.' But he knew exactly where his dad was going with this. Alexei was his friend. An exotic novelty when they'd first met, with his tales of capercaillie shooting and vodka drinking, but the bond between them had become something more substantial in the last weeks of term. Meaningful, even. Now, though, all that stood for nothing. *Are you a patriot, Noah?* Their final conversation at school had not been what it seemed. Subterfuge masquerading as friendship, another agenda at work.

'After I was recruited, it was always Moscow's intention to recruit you one day too,' his dad continued. 'They're big believers in father–son relationships. But they were wary. It wasn't your website or technical skills, or your bookish interest in espionage, all of which they much admired, but your... well, whether you had what it took to be a spy – in the field.'

'You mean if I was hench enough.'

Noah was too busy trying to process the implications of Alexei's approach, and the strange pride he felt at being deemed worth recruiting by the SVR, to be offended by any insults about his physique. He was used to them. Alexei had been particularly cruel, always trying to toughen him up, challenging him to late-night press-up contests, games of knuckles...

'The Russians can be very black and white when it comes to their spies. Being cerebral is fine, providing that comes with muscle.'

'I'd have thought my politics would have been more of a problem,' Noah said. 'I've not exactly expressed support for Putin.'

'No?'

'Absolutely not. Particularly after Syria. And then the whole US election thing.'

'What about that school essay you wrote last term, about the way the Western media misreports Russia? And your suggestion that we should all watch RT News for a bit, just to get a different perspective?'

'I was playing devil's advocate,' Noah protested. How did his dad know about that? 'Half of the class was told to write from one point of view, the other half from–'

'Alexei omitted to tell his father that bit when he sent him a copy of your essay. He's desperate for his "crazy British friend" to work for the Russians. For the motherland. The essay was enough to convince him and his father that you might be of the same political persuasion as me, might follow in my treacherous footsteps.'

'Why didn't they just ask you to approach me directly?'

'They did. But of course that was more problematic for me than they realised. First I would have had to tell you that I worked for MI5, then explain that I was working for the Russians but as a double agent. That's quite a lot for a teenager to take in out of the blue. So I told them it would be better if you found out for yourself. Over time, in the field, with some sort of context. They liked the idea, because it also gave them the chance to see what you're made of. To test you.'

'Test me?' Noah thought back over the past few tumultuous days, his heart sinking. 'You mean when Alexei asked me to find the mole it was just a test?' He spat out the last word like snake venom, unable to disguise the disappointment – the disdain – in his voice. He had been played. By his Russian roommate and friend. This holiday hadn't felt like a game. It had been very real, particularly the kicking he'd received on the way up to Nare Head. And Sasha, dying in front of him on the lawn…

'As I say, I felt it would be best if you found out about me for yourself. And, yes, they were testing you too. A test that you've passed with flying colours, I should add. They've also been impressed with Clemmie. Valeria doesn't often meet her match.'

They both looked at Clemmie on Nare Head, where she was now sitting, knees drawn up, staring out across the bay towards Portscatho.

'What about Sasha? Was he being tested too?'

'I'm afraid they'd already made up their minds about him long before you came on the scene. He's been viewed as a security risk for some time. Dead man walking. You're not to blame for what they did to him. Far from it. As I understand, he's likely to make a full recovery, thanks to the information you gave the paramedics. Fortunately, the Russians don't know it was you who told them that Sasha might have been poisoned with *Gelsemium*.'

'And "James Hilton"? The guy who died at the hotel?'

His dad flinched. 'More problematic, I'm afraid.' He rose from the bench and walked to the cliff edge. Noah stood up and followed him. 'The fella was an investigative journalist,' he continued. 'Freelance, undercover, sniffing around the Home Secretary. Moscow was nervous. Thought he might be on to Kreshensky. Me.'

'So they just *killed* him?'

'We don't know exactly how he died. *Gelsemium* too, probably. It's important you are aware of the world you are entering, Noah. The people we are dealing with here. Many journalists have been killed in Russia.'

Noah knew about some of them, people like Anna Politkovskaya, murdered for her critical reporting of Chechnya.

He'd written about her on his website. There were many others too. He thought of the man in the sauna, the way he had approached him at the cocktail party earlier in the evening, appealing to his interest in espionage. *Good to have another set of eyes and ears on the ground. No need to mention our conversation to your parents. To anyone, actually.* He had been an undercover journalist whose cover story was spying. There was a certain irony in that.

'When I saw you meeting Kreshensky,' Noah said, still thinking of the dead man's open eyes, 'I could have just got on my phone, posted a photo to my blog and exposed you as a spy.'

'Could you?' His dad let the question linger. Noah knew now in his heart that he could never have betrayed him, his own father. 'As I say, the Russians place a lot of faith in fathers and sons. So do I. They believe it's more important than anything else. They figured you wouldn't.'

'But I might have done…'

'They made a judgement call.'

'I could have blown the whole operation apart.'

His dad paused. Was he deciding how much to tell him? 'Let's just say there were contingencies in place. I'm not sure if you tried your phone at St Just – all local comms were knocked out, including landlines, even at the hotel, an hour before we met. They still are, and they won't be restored until I give the Russians the all-clear that you are onside.'

Noah pulled out his mobile. He normally got a signal up here, but sure enough it was saying 'no service'.

'What about Clemmie?' he asked.

'She's more complicated.'

Tell me about it, Noah thought.

'She wasn't meant to be with you at St Just. The plan was for Valeria to neutralise her in the church at St Anthony, but it seems she met her match in Clemmie.'

'Wait a minute – "neutralise"? Like they neutralised James Hilton in the sauna?'

'No. Just stop her from coming with you to St Just. So now the Russians are assuming that she saw me with Kreshensky and they need you to explain to her what I was doing there.'

'And how do they propose I do that?'

They both glanced across at Clemmie again, still sitting on the rock.

'The Russians never operate without insurance,' his dad began. 'They want you to tell Clemmie that if she breathes a word of this to anyone, they will destroy her father with *kompromat* – compromising material about the British Home Secretary that we know they have been compiling over the past few months. They hope they won't have to go down this route. In fact, they rate Clemmie very highly – as we do – and believe that one day she can be turned too. Maybe even her father as well. They have great faith in your powers of persuasion.'

Noah didn't like the idea of Clemmie being blackmailed into silence.

'Is any of it true?' he asked. 'The compromising material?' He knew all about *kompromat*, thanks to the Kremlin's interest in Donald Trump.

'Not as far we're aware, but they're not afraid to make things up, as you know. *Vranyo*. Shameless lying. His dad paused. 'I've spoken to MacKenzie. As Home Secretary, he'd already been briefed on the operation, of course, knew about my double role, the Russians' potential interest in you. He's not happy that Clemmie has been caught up in the whole affair, but I've told him you'll look after her.'

'Can I tell her? The truth? I don't want her going around thinking you're a traitor.'

'Only when you've both signed the Official Secrets Act.'

Noah wondered what she would say. Perhaps she had already guessed where his dad's real sympathies lay. Either way, he would always be grateful for her loyalty, her pledge not to go public. He still wasn't sure what he would have done if MacKenzie had been the one who had met Kreshensky.

'You know, we thought her dad might have been the mole. Can you believe it?' he said, trying to make light of a thought that had haunted him day and night.

'What on earth gave you that idea?'

Noah wasn't sure any more, couldn't remember where any of this had started.

'He's a guest at the hotel. He ordered a copy of *Superyacht Monthly*. And he's been reading a book about Cornish churches, the church at St Anthony-in-Roseland. And...'

His dad smiled. 'That's what happens when the wrong dots are joined.'

'How do you mean?'

'MacKenzie visited Pendennis Shipyard this morning. It's a big employer in Falmouth – more than three hundred and seventy people work there. Building and refitting superyachts. And tomorrow he's giving a talk to a local charity, the Cornwall Historic Churches Trust – it's a big fundraising lunch, organised by Toby Ashworth's wife, Katie. She's a hotshot lawyer and doesn't suffer fools gladly. MacKenzie and I were comparing diaries earlier. He likes to turn up well briefed for these sort of events.'

Noah smiled to himself. He couldn't wait to tell Clemmie. 'Do the Russians know we're talking now?' he asked.

'They think you're confronting me, an angry and confused teenager, before hearing me out, listening to my reasons for meeting Kreshensky. We talk politics, agree that Russia is misunderstood by an imperialist West that wishes to police the world, and applaud the way it took the lead against ISIS in the Syrian conflict and its refreshing desire to reset relations with America. We finish with you agreeing to support your father in his important work because you love him, even more than Russian sons love their fathers.'

Noah swallowed hard. 'And what are we actually doing?'

His dad paused, which was always a portent of something. 'The Russians aren't the only ones who want to recruit you.'

He turned to look at his dad, who was smiling. A proud smile that seemed to rise up from deep within him.

'Your friendship with Alexei opens up new channels for us,' his dad said. 'There are many children of powerful Russian politicians and businessmen in Britain's public schools. We need people like you.'

His dad put an arm around him, pulling him in towards him, just as he used to do when Noah was younger. He didn't resist. He let his head rest on his dad's shoulder. They hadn't hugged for a long time.

'There would be more tests first, from our side this time, but we believe you've got what it takes to be a pure dead brilliant spy.' He gave Noah another squeeze. 'And between you and me, we want to recruit Clemmie too. You make a good team. Just don't tell her father. Not yet.'

Noah felt a warm glow spread through his body. Him and Clemmie. Clementine bloody MacKenzie. The most beautiful girl in his school. The love of his life.

His dad stood up and looked out to sea. Their bus had finally arrived.

'See you back at the hotel,' he said.

'Cream tea?' Noah asked.

'I think we've earned one, don't you?' And with that he set off running towards Portloe.

Noah bit his lip as he watched his dad go, not sure whether to laugh or cry. He was about to say something, how much he loved his dad, perhaps, or ask if his grandpa knew (he was sure he did), but no words would come. Instead, he turned to look across at Clemmie and smiled, thinking of the future that lay ahead of them.

THE END

Acknowledgements

THE PUBLISHER would like to thank the following individuals, businesses and organisations for helping to make this book possible. As is typical in the spy world not everyone may have been aware of their involvement, but others have been very aware and helpful, going out of their way to source the detail needed for such a book. Of course, Jon Stock's enthusiasm and imagination for spycraft is irresistibly infectious and it has been an absolute pleasure to watch, listen and learn from a master whilst he creates his work. It should be made mandatory on European motorways to listen to a Jon Stock audible book, which I guarantee will reduce the apparent journey time by at least fifty per cent. One's education is incomplete if you have not read his spy thriller trilogy, starting with *Dead Spy Running*. Hilary, his wife, has been a great support and a super-efficient forensic photographer, capturing all the subtle details on research missions into spy land, and I know the author relied heavily on the accuracy of her intel. Apart from that they are simply a great fun couple and have been an absolute joy to work with in the production of *To Snare A Spy*.

I am very conscious that without the permission and help from Mrs N Grant-Dalton the beautifully set scenes in and around Place House and Church would not have been included. I am therefore indebted to the Grant-Dalton family and their Spry ancestry for the forthcoming historical information. With typical custodial pride, she quite rightly pointed out that 'if a few more people do visit the dear little church and pop something in the donation box then all the better'. If you are unable to visit this church, or the equally charming St Just-in-Roseland Church with its steep, creek-side garden, then please do consider supporting the Cornwall Historic Churches Trust, whose steadfast fundraising work helps to restore and maintain many similar pre-loved and discreet churches all around Cornwall.

For the very latest awe-inspiring maritime technical innovations, then, Pendennis Shipyard is hard to beat. With many thanks to Toby Allies, marketing director, for the insight and possibilities for the latest bespoke lines in superyachts. There is simply nowhere else better to recommend for your next superyacht refit!

On a smaller scale but no less important, thanks go to Simon and Susie, who look after *Alice Rose* and her guests so beautifully; Colin at Smugglers' Cottage; and the team at Falmouth Boat Construction for tending to *Alice Rose*'s every need and cosseting her during the winter.

Much of the book is set in and around The Nare Hotel, and it is with infinite patience and subtle amusement that the staff provided essential country house charm and comfort through their traditional and attentive service to the author and many guests alike. Several have provided rich background detail from the other side of the green baize door. There are many long-term members of staff who have been very loyal and deserve named thanks: Ken (Father of the House, head barman and raconteur), Julie (assistant manageress), Barbara (maître d'), Paul (restaurant manager), Liz (housekeeper), Alex (dining room), from reception Wendy, Jessica, Julia, Margret, and Caroline; and Karl (head gardener); but there are still many other unnamed loyalists who could equally join this list. It is probably easier to come and meet them and decide for yourself who your favourite is. They are the heart and soul of The Nare. I thank them all.

I would like to thank Kate Wild for introducing me to Jon Stock and many other journalists who I have had the pleasure of hosting at the hotel, and also Georgie, Maddi, Aimee and her dedicated PR team at Wild West in Truro. They do a fantastic job. Likewise our marketing associations with Small Luxury Hotels of the World, Rebecca Recommends in America, and Pride of Britain Hotels.

Thanks should also be extended to the hotel's many local suppliers, whose regional produce enhances the Cornish experience. To Rodda's Clotted Cream and Tregothnan Estate's tea plantation for the essential ingredients of The Nare's delicious afternoon Cornish cream tea. To St Austell Brewery for copious supplies of Taittinger and Tribute. To our local farmers for their prime joints of Cornish beef and lamb. To our several fish merchants, not least Perran Seafoods and Wing of St Mawes, for their oh-so-fresh supplies of seafood. A properly run country house by the sea would be seriously compromised without the loyal support of an army of local suppliers.

To Daphne Burt, fellow director, my grandmother's loyal confidant, manageress, and an integral part of our family in all but name for more years than I have been born, I offer my sincere thanks and appreciation. I recognise her years of wisdom, guidance and loyalty, without which the story of The Nare would not have existed.

Finally to my wife, Katie, director, embedded lawyer, manuscript speed-reader extraordinaire, enabler of fun, and Minister without Portfolio, I am eternally grateful.

As a gesture we will be making a modest donation from book sales to the two charities we are both involved with: firstly, the aforementioned Cornwall Historic Churches, and secondly, the Cornwall Community Foundation, which helps many different striving communities who do not have the good fortune to benefit from four-star-hotel luxury and the stunning surroundings of the Roseland Peninsula. Regrettably there are too many impoverished communities who require such need in Cornwall, so this donation really can only be seen as a token effort.

THE AUTHOR would like to thank Toby Ashworth for the free rein he has given me in writing this book. It is my sixth spy thriller and I can say, with hand on heart, that I have had more fun researching and writing this thriller than I've had working on any other book. It was always going to be an entertaining project from the moment Toby's extension number – 007, of course – flashed up on my mobile phone. Toby is a first-rate hotelier but he would make an equally effective spymaster. I have been coming to Cornwall all my life, but when I saw the county refracted through his covert lens, it became an even more thrilling place, full of intrigue and adventure.

I'd also like to thank Toby's wife, Katie, and their two children, Cordy and Gee, for welcoming me into their home, hosting me so generously and coming up with such good ideas for the book. Katie's reading of the manuscript was invaluable and her suggestions spot on – just what I'd expect from 'a hotshot lawyer', as Noah's dad refers to her.

All the staff at The Nare have made me feel at home during my various residencies, most of them spent in the Lemoria Suite, which was an inspiring place to write, even when basking sharks weren't swimming past my window. They have been very generous with their time, sharing life stories and hotel experiences, as well as answering my odd questions. Not everyone knew, at the beginning, that I was writing a spy thriller. On one occasion, I asked Andrew, a concierge, how long it would take him to unlock the hotel's front door at midnight if, say, I had run up from the beach, where I had been chased in the dark by someone, and was frantically ringing the bell. He paused for a moment before asking, ever so politely, 'Is everything alright, Mr Stock?'

I am indebted to my superb copy-editor, Lucy Ridout, and eagle-eyed proofreader, Averill Buchanan, both of whom have saved my blushes, whether it's spotting narrative inconsistencies or stray commas or much worse. Thanks, too, to Nick Hill who has drawn the beautiful and informative map at the front of the book. I'd also like to thank TJ INK and Wild West for all their help and professionalism, and a special word of gratitude to my Glaswegian father-in-law, Stewart McLennan, who patiently answered my questions about Scotland. Any vernacular mistakes are mine.

Finally, thank you to my wonderful wife, Hilary, my first and best reader, a fine photographer and always so supportive, and to our three children, all of whom have helped with this book. Skateboarding, teenage text speak, web proxies – they're the go-to team. Unlike Noah, they haven't had the tap on the shoulder yet, but it can only be a matter of time.

POSTSCRIPT

Lest we forget. We will remember them.

THE LATE STAFF SERGEANT OLAF SCHMID GC was killed in Afghanistan in October 2009. He was a former silver-service waiter in the dining room at The Nare, where his mother, Barbara, is our maître d'.

Olaf's nickname was Oz and it is entirely appropriate that a bomb disposal sniffer dog, sponsored by Barbara, has been named in his memory. Oz, a German short-haired pointer, features in *To Snare A Spy*, when he comes to check the hotel for bombs in advance of a visit by the Home Secretary. He recognises Barbara as he enters the sitting room during afternoon tea.

In Olaf's brief time at The Nare before joining the army and gaining the coveted green beret (awarded only to those completing the Commando course), he was renowned for his immaculate turnout and somehow managing to make The Nare waiter's rather plain uniform appear as crisp as a military tunic. It is heart-warming that Olaf's presence is still felt and remembered with affection, and that many guests return showing sympathy and respect for his mother, one of The Nare's most longstanding and dedicated members of staff.

Olaf's memory lives on in Oz, a real-life bomb detection dog, and, we hope, in the fictitious hound who features in *To Snare A Spy*. Oz's potential was spotted by Inspector David Eddy, who is in charge of dogs on Tri Force Operations for Wiltshire, Gloucestershire and Avon & Somerset Police. Inspector Eddy recently explained how Oz came to be named: 'We had previously asked for some suggestions for the puppy's name through Twitter and Facebook and had received some excellent ideas. Olaf Schmid was suggested as soon as we identified the puppy as a potential explosives search dog.

'In the circumstances, naming a bomb detection dog after a decorated bomb disposal officer seemed to be the most appropriate choice and we were able to contact Olaf's mother and she agreed to us naming Oz in honour of her son. We have set up a Twitter account – @TriForceOzzy – to allow everyone to follow his exploits on his journey towards becoming an operational police dog.'

Hector, Izzy and Jenga, The Nare Hotel Hounds, are now following their new hero's progress on social media – their Twitter handle is @HotelHounds. Other hounds are also welcome to join in the conversation. Good luck, Oz.

Tragically, Olaf's luck ran out at the end of October 2009. The citation that accompanied his posthumous George Cross graphically illustrates his bravery and heroism. We print it here in full, in memory of a remarkable soldier and son.

THE AWARD OF THE GEORGE CROSS TO STAFF SERGEANT OLAF SCHMID

Staff Sergeant Schmid was a High Threat Improvised Explosive Device Disposal (IEDD) Operator in Helmand from June 2009 until his death in action on 31 October 2009.

He deployed at the height of Operation Panchai Palang (Panther's Claw) and went immediately into the fray, into one of the most physically draining, mentally intense and hazardous jobs in Helmand. Typically having to deploy on foot, thereby precluding the option of specialist protective equipment and severely limiting the use of remote controlled vehicles, he spent long periods of time in close proximity to Victim Operated IEDs (VOIED) and in gravest personal danger. Before his death in action he responded to 42 IED tasks, personally dealing with 70 confirmed IEDs. A number of examples illustrate his bravery.

An infantry company based in Wishtan province was isolated by a substantial minefield, and the infamous Pharmacy Road, the only resupply route, was blocked by a medium-wheeled tractor and another vehicle, both blown up by very large IEDs. Intelligence, unenviable first-hand experience and numerous unexplained explosions from the area indicated that the area of the stricken vehicles was laced with IEDs. At 0800 hours on 9 August 2009, as temperatures soared past 45 degrees Celsius, Schmid started work. Within only a hundred metres he found and cleared an IED, and once within 100 metres of the vehicles, intent on using a remote controlled vehicle (RCV) and remote explosive clearance devices, he deployed an RCV that struck an IED and was destroyed. Schmid moved forward without hesitation and, well inside the most lethal arc of any device, manually placed explosive charges, clearing a route to within five metres of the vehicles.

His team then moved to clear a compound adjacent to the stricken vehicles to drag them off the road. When a second IED was found, Schmid made another manual approach and rapidly got rid of it. A new approach to the vehicles from the compound was explosively created for the hulks to be dragged clear. Schmid painstakingly cleared up to both vehicles and his first trip took an hour. He was relying on his eyesight and understanding of enemy tactics alone. Despite the threat, Schmid again decided against explosive clearance; time was critical so he placed heavy and cumbersome chains onto the stricken vehicles, the riskiest of enterprises given the very high likelihood of booby traps, and the vehicles were finally dragged clear. As light started to fade, Schmid then personally led a high-risk clearance of the road where the vehicles had been manually disposing of two further IEDs. The clearance had lasted 11 hours. It was physically, mentally and emotionally draining, but the road was open and the company resupplied. The resounding success of this battlegroup operation was entirely due to the heroic, selfless acts of Schmid.

On 8 October 2009 Schmid was tasked in Sangin District Centre to deal with an artillery shell reported by unmentored Afghan National Army (ANA) soldiers. On arrival the ANA led him, unsuspecting, directly to the device. He was now not only at grave personal risk but immediately realised that the many unsuspecting civilians around him in the bustling bazaar were also in peril. Time was not on his side. He quickly assessed that the shell was in fact part of a live Radio Controlled IED intended to cause maximum casualties in a well-populated area. The nature of the device also meant it was almost certainly over-watched by the bomber controlling it. Without any consideration for his own safety, Schmid immediately decided to neutralise the IED manually. To do this he knew he was employing a render-safe procedure that should only ever be employed in the gravest of circumstances and which is conducted at the highest personal risk to the operator. In an instant, Schmid made the most courageous decision possible, consciously placing his own life on the line in order to save the lives of countless Afghan civilians and demonstrating bravery of the highest order and well beyond the call of duty.

At the end of October 2009 Schmid was involved in an operation near Forward Operating Base Jackson in Battle Group North's area. Having dealt with three IEDs already that day, Schmid and his team were transiting to another compound when a searcher discovered a command wire running down the alleyway they were using. Schmid and his team were trapped in the alleyway with no safe route forward or back as they did not know in which direction the IED was situated. Knowing that his team were in potential danger, he immediately took action to reduce the hazard. Schmid eventually traced the wire to a complex command wire IED in that it incorporated three linked buried main charges. He was killed whilst dealing with the device. Schmid's actions on that fateful day, when trapped in an alleyway with no safe means of escape, probably saved the lives of his team.

These occasions are representative of the complexity and danger that Schmid had faced daily throughout his four-month tour. His selfless gallantry, his devotion to duty, and his indefatigable courage displayed time and time again saved countless military and civilian lives and is worthy of the highest recognition.

For more information about the The Felix Fund, the bomb disposal charity that supports victims and families, and Barbara's chosen charity to support, please contact:

Felix Fund – the bomb disposal charity
Vauxhall Barracks
Foxhall Road
Didcot
Oxon
OX11 7ES

Tel: 07713 752901
www.felixfund.org.uk